S.R. Bissette

THE PALEO PATH

Paleo and the History of Dinosaur Comics

I.

For those of us who grew up aching for a dinosaur comic uncluttered by intrusive human characters, or anthropomorphized talking saurians, *Paleo* is a joy, a revelation, a little slice of heaven we can hold in our hands and revisit time and again. It's what we've wanted since before we could clearly speak. *Paleo* is a time machine, a window back into a primordial world populated by glorious creatures we know walked the Earth eons before us. *Paleo* is an honest-to-God "dinosaur comic," and an impeccable one at that and, best of all, it is now under one cover in book form.

This is undoubtedly Jim Lawson's most ambitious, personal, and polished work to date, building upon his already considerable creations and credentials, from his first published solo comic book series, *Bade Biker*, to his most recent graphic novel collaboration with Peter Laird, *Planet Racers*. *Paleo* is Jim's finest work to date, with a breadth and depth of emotional intensity, clarity, and range that is intoxicating. Jim breathes life into these creatures and doesn't just put them through their paces: he walks in their footsteps, breathes the air they breathe, sinks his teeth into these glimpses of their lives as surely as they bury their choppers into one another.

Mind you, "choppers" of a very different kind are more typical of the comics normally associated with Jim, which is as sly a lead-in to a brief discussion of Jim's past. Although comicdom -- the industry, such as it is, and the comics press, such as it isn't -- has somehow seen fit to by-and-large ignore Jim's prolific output, the fact is that he has produced more pages of the *Teenage Mutant Ninja Turtles* comic book than any other artist, and an entire generation of comic readers have grown up with his work. Another generation is currently cutting its comic book-

reflected more vividly in his other comics work. Lawson's love of cartooning and motorcycles marked his early comics work (particularly *Bade Biker*) as a fresh permutation of the "Custom Car Culture" cartooning tradition that emerged from the West Coast, characterized by Big Daddy Roth's drag-racing and biking monsters (led by the immortal Rat Fink) and popular 1960's-to-present comics zines like Pete Peterson's *CARtoons* and *BIKEtoons*. Jim's sleek, clean, energetic work eschews the fly-blown vibrating "meat 'n heat" aesthetic of the Roth hot-rod-surfer-biker monster menagerie, but Lawson's roots are definitely there (and he has had drawings published in the Peterson zines to prove it). Telling, though, that Jim's characteristic precision line work (which for me echoes elements of *MAD* artist Paul Coker's style) doesn't seem sterile: you can still feel the grit, smell the hot metal, feel the heat. Jim's line is alive, as are his characters. And especially his dinosaurs.

Paleo is a genuine dinosaur comic, a rare thing.

But *Paleo* is hardly the first of its kind -- any more than Ricardo Delgado's *Age of Reptiles,* or my own stab at the form, *S.R. Bissette's Tyrant,* were the first of their kind -- and it won't be the last.

Stephen R. Bissette Art - *From S.R. Bissette's Tyrant #4, Winter, 1996. SpiderBaby Graphics and Publications.*

There were dinosaur comics before *Paleo*, and the new high-water mark that *Paleo* represents will no doubt inspire others to build further on these not-yet-ossified bones.

Understand, however, that a true dinosaur comic is something unique, unblemished by human characters.

Jim doesn't need a "lost world," "lost island," time machine, or atom-age mutations stomping cities into dust. Forget such spectacles before entering the world of *Paleo*. Forget about *Rip Hunter, Time Master* or *Gorgo* or *Konga*. Forget *Godzilla, King of the Monsters*. These comics indeed feature dinosaurs but they are not true dinosaur comics.

II.

The precursors were, of course, the dinosaur *artists*. These were the illustrators and painters who first put pencil, pen, and brush to paper or canvas and fleshed out the fossil reconstructions to create panoramas of what the prehistoric world must have, might have, maybe was like. Prominent among these is the pioneer Charles R. Knight, who established the field almost single-handedly in the very early 1900's. Working hand-in-glove with the premiere paleontologists of his day, Knight was the first "pop paleo artist." His vivid reconstructions of prehistoric life graced the walls of museums (such as Chicago's Field Museum), the pages of

George Turner art - from "The Ancient Greek Plains" (1951) as it appears in Spawn Of Skull Island by Michael H. Price, George Turner and Orville Goldner, 2002, Luminary Press.

books, periodicals, and journals, and became the standard illustrations for school and home texts like the *Encyclopedia Britannica* and *National Geographic*. Others followed in Knight's footsteps: Rudolph Zallinger in the U.S., Zdenak Burian in Czechoslovakia, and many others. Many have grown up in the thrall of William Stout's marvelous prehistoric creations, or marveled at the work of the exquisite paleontological artists who rose to prominence in the 1980's and early 1990's. But Knight's paintings and drawings were the wellspring from which all dinosaur imagery flowed, and countless illustrators and cartoonists have done little more but slavishly copy Knight's work for generations.

The ache, then, for many, was the urge to see Knight's paintings move -- or at least enjoy a fuller life on the page. That urge impelled

pioneer stop-motion animator Willis O'Brien to bring dinosaurs to life on the big screen (*The Lost World, King Kong*, etc.), just as it moved his teenage successor Ray Harryhausen to labor over his own never-completed epic *Evolution* before graduating to continuing O'Brien's legacy in films like *Beast From 20,000 Fathoms*. The same urge drove Disney Studio cartoon animators to create the memorable "Rites of Spring" sequence for *Fantasia*, and cartoonists like Joe Kubert or Ross Andru and Mike Esposito to sneak dinosaurs into every comic book job they could. Thus, Kubert's *Green Lantern* and Andru and Esposito's *Wonder Woman* and *Star-Spangled War Stories* (where G.I.'s fought living dinosaurs) but these weren't dinosaur comics – they were comics with dinosaurs. The dinosaurs were props, cameo villains, guest-stars; they weren't the stars of their own stories, as Knight had portrayed them in his evocative tableaus.

McCay's *Dreams of a Rarebit Fiend* featured the occasional dinosaur. *Alley Oop*, though, was not a dinosaur comic. Even though Alley Oop and his kin cavorted with dinosaurs (including Oop's faithful brontosaurian steed, Dinny), *Alley Oop* was not, *per se*, a dinosaur comic. Like most prehistoric novels, comics, and movies, Hamlin's comic was set in a fantasy universe where men and dinosaurs co-habitated.

Between 1951 and 1952, Texan George E. Turner crafted a regionally-published weekly comic strip, *The Ancient Great Plains*, for the Amarillo-based *Sunday News-Globe*. Working under the guidance of West Texas State College geology professor Dr. Roy H. Reinhart, Turner undertook nothing less than a painstakingly illustrated science comic strip detailing the evolution of life in his home state, rich with the myriad forms of flora and fauna that swam, slithered, stalked and soared across millions of years. Turner's love of films colored the and his reconstructions were often drawn from the work of Knight and others. Nevertheless,

Jesse Marsh art - from Dinosaurs! (Dell Movie Classic #1120)1960, Dell Publishing Co., Inc.

his work had its own flavor, and one cannot help but be struck by the accomplishments showcased in the sampler of *The Ancient Great Plains* offered by Turner's longtime writing partner Michael H. Price in the revised edition of Turner and Orville Goldner's King Kong book, *Spawn of Skull Island*. This is, very likely, the first true American dinosaur comic. Jesse Marsh illustrated what might be the first dinosaur pin-ups in Dell's long-running comic book series adapted from Edgar Rice Burroughs' *Tarzan*. These appeared shortly after the series' maiden dinosaur epic , "The Valley of the Monsters," from *Tarzan* #7, released in 1949. The science was dubious at best, and the saurians were graced with Burroughs' (and comic book writer Gaylord Du Bois') resonant invented monikers for familiar dinosaurs -- tyrannosaurs were "garths," triceratops were "gryfs," pterosaurs were "thidpars," etc. These were the creatures that roamed the lost land of Pal-Ul-Don, in which "The Valley of the Monsters" was nestled. Here, dinosaurs still roamed and the surrounding tribal people bred their unusual mounts: three-horned gryfs, wingless dyals, and other antediluvian creatures. From its earliest installments, almost every issue of *Tarzan*

Jesse Marsh art - from Tarzan #33, Jun. 1952. Dell Publishing Co., Inc.

offered single-page pin-ups offering tidbits of lore about Tarzan's world, including the reptilian monsters of Pal-Ul-Don.

Though it was and is fashionable to debunk Marsh's comic art as primitive, he remains one of the true masters of his era -- and no comic artist before Marsh ever rendered animals with such tactile, believable life. His depictions of African and imaginary animal life were quite realistic. His gryfs, garths, thidpars and dyals were utterly lifelike in an oddly blunt, pragmatic, primal way that lent gravity to the wildest of Du Bois' Burroughs-inspired scripts. The dinosaurs of other Dell comics -- Alex Toth's efficient but unconvincing saurians for comic book adaptations of the science fiction films *The Land Unknown* and *The Lost World*, and the uncredited artist who illustrated the comic version of Irwin Allen's documentary *The Animal World* -- seemed pale indeed in the shadow of Marsh's meaty saurians, including his work on Dell's movie comic *Dinosaurs!* from 1960. However fleeting,

Jesse Marsh art - from Tarzan #110, Jan. - Feb. 1959. Dell Publishing Co. Inc.

3

his single-page strips featuring dinosaurs in their own time and/or environment were savored snapshots of a dinosaur comic that might have been -- but wasn't.

Contemporary with the early issues and success of Du Bois and Marsh's *Tarzan* series for Dell, Joe Kubert followed suit in a more ambitious manner in his *Tor* comics series, which debuted in *1,000,000 Years B.C.* in 1953. Kubert's "straight, no-chaser" revamp of *Alley Oop* was dead-serious and brimming with action, and from its first issue featured one-page solo portraits of the dinosaurs Kubert anachronistically co-starred with his titular caveman hero. Kubert also scribed more ambitious informational narrative pieces, such as "The Story of Evolution" (in *3-D Tor*), detailing the development of the Wooly Mammoth.

Along with Kubert's distinctively muscular pen, brush, and ink renditions were the comparatively static, precision dinosaur illustrations by Russ Heath. These dinosaur portraits were beautifully done, the tidbits of paleontological info in the captions lending verisimilitude to the entirety of Kubert's prehistoric fantasy. But these still weren't comics narratives. The key sequential narratives in *Tor* were dedicated to Tor's adventures, and those of a modern boy whose dreams plunge him into the imaginary caveman-and-dinosaur era. Thus, the short science features and one-pagers were again glimpses of a dinosaur comic that "could have been." Kubert's later return to *Tor* -- in the pages of his adventurous but short-lived 1976 publishing experiment *Sojourn* and his later *Tor* revival for Marvel Comics' second Epic Comics line, "Heavy Hitters," in 1993 -- was leaner, meaner, and brimming with violent action featuring dinosaurs and wholly imaginary primordial creatures, but it still wasn't a true dinosaur comic.

III.

The first true dinosaur comics to appear regularly on the newsstand evolved within a title that was arguably inspired by *Tor*, one that fused the increasingly popular western comics genre with the lively "caveman-and-dinos" universe. Dell Comics' *Turok, Son of Stone* debuted in 1954 in *Dell Four Color #596*. Two Indian braves, *Turok* and Ander are trapped in a remote "lost valley" in the American west, a place where they would remain for over two decades. Artist Fred Greenberg once described *Turok* as "the first existential comic" and he's right; *Turok* and Ander were forever trapped in their lost valley, and knew they'd never escape, but had to keep

Rex Maxon art - from Turok, Son Of Stone #8, Jun. - Aug. 1957, Dell Publishing Co., Inc.

trying to find a way out nevertheless. The debut issue was drawn by *Tarzan* comic strip artist Rex Maxon, who occasionally returned to the series. Maxon's steady and lasting contribution to *Turok* – and to comics history and the evolution of the dinosaur comic genre -- was launched without fanfare in *Turok #8*. Maxon's stint on this first *Turok* adventure featured a T. rex clearly patterned after the portly blue carnosaur in a Rudolph Zallinger painting, but Maxon's brisk, lively art for the rest of his *Turok* tenure (particularly the "Young Earth" stories) did not slavishly rely upon his reference files, nor did he succumb to the temptation to lend his prehistoric creatures expressive faces contrary to their true natures and forms. This skill came to the fore in Maxon's delineation of issue #8's four-page back-up strip, "Danger at the Nest," in which a mother Pteranodon defends her treetop nest from a raiding Dimetrodon. The uncredited script -- presumably by series writer Paul S. Newman -- was a model of efficient, unpretentious storytelling, and Maxon's artwork rendered its prehistoric creatures without a hint of anthropomorphizing. But within this simple narrative, something unique was born: this was not an illustrated text page, or dressed-out pop science tidbit, but a fully-realised narrative. The fusion of text captions and sequential art told the tale with direct economy, clarity, and mounted genuine suspense without cheating. Note, too, the spare but elegant use of just two word balloons, used not to lend the pterosaurs speech, but to indicate the sound the mother makes feigning injury to lure the predator away from her nest -- a cry echoed neatly by her hatchlings' call for food in the final panel. Thus, the "sound" evoked by the use of just two word balloons enhanced the kinetic "you are there" immediacy of the strip. Furthermore, in both text and art, these were animals acting like, and presented as, *animals*. Without stretching believability or relying on the sort of devices comics usually required in stories involving animals (i.e., human narrators, framing panels featuring human characters, lending speech or human thought to the animal protagonists, etc.), the writer invited the reader to empathize with these creatures, particularly the protagonist. Sly references are made to emotions, but none so emphatically as to break the spell. This mother Pteranodon "proudly eyes her first young breaking his shell...," "...realizes she cannot fight off the lumbering reptile -- her only hope is to lure him away...," "...cleverly back[s] away, just out of his range...," "...as she is about to fly off triumphantly, her wing is caught...," "...sees with relief the Dimetrodon hunting far from her nest...," and "...wonders how her first hatched young is making out..." Even the ravenous carnivore is afforded a moment of empathy, as he "eagerly" scrabbles toward his prey. Thus, for the first time, prehistoric animals moving within their own environment were shown interacting, capable of a range of emotions -- pride, calculation, hope, cleverness, triumph, disappointment, relief, wonder – yet rendered in primal enough terms to remain animals.

Note that, at the time, "Danger in the Nest" was just another experiment. For a couple of issues, *Turok*'s editor had toyed with various approaches to fleshing out each issue with the tried-and-true single-page informative pieces (inside cover sequential pieces, illustrated text pieces). The first back-up strip was "Lotor Goes House Hunting" in #7, in which a mother raccoon seeks shelter for her brood amid a flood in the "lost valley," stalked by hungry saurians. It was a step in the right direction, but still relied on the blatant appeal of a somewhat anachronistic furry warm-blooded mammal protagonist (admittedly a clear step away from human protagonists, but not by much) anthropomorphized by the writer ("'It's vacant! Come on in!' Mother Raccoon chirrups happily...."). "Danger in the Nest" eschewed such devices with neat abandon, assuming the reader could and would empathize with a cold-blooded (as it was presumed all prehistoric reptiles were, at that time) protagonist without reliance on Beatrix Potter-like, or Aesopian, conceits.

Turok's editor realized they were on to something, as Newman and Maxon were back in the very next issue, working with even greater assurance in the four-page "The Plight of the Plesiosaur." A wounded young Plesiosaur's hunting skills are compromised by his injury; he seeks and finds plentiful fresh-water prey inland, until the intrusion of a hungry Tyrannosaurus rex drives him back out to sea. Again, the suspense generated was genuine, and the situation and characterizations (Maxon again makes his animals seem nothing more, or less, than living animals, but they are indeed characters) believable throughout. The slight imposition to the final panel of a moral appropriate to the Eisenhower era ("...some instinct of self-preservation tells the Plesiosaur that the open sea is where he belongs...") did not compromise the modest accomplishment of the narrative, any more than the completely bogus paleontology did (typically placing species which were separated from one another by millions of years and tens of thousands of miles, being from different geological eras and geographic regions; a failing of almost all dinosaur comics, yesterday and today).

What was important -- and fresh -- was that the conjectured behavior of the dinosaurs and prehistoric creatures was convincing at a gut level. Shorn of the need to artificially inflate these incredible animals into the stature of monsters, interact with anachronistic human beings, or motivate them to attack contemporary metropolitan areas, Newman and Maxon were free -- for the first time in comics history, or, for that matter, arguably any medium outside of science and pop science texts -- to portray prehistoric animals as animals. These new kinds of stories relied upon extrapolating possible behaviors for the extinct creatures from that of contemporary life forms: a mother Pteranodon behaving like a protective bird, a hungry plesiosaur seeking easier feeding grounds. Though the writer and cartoonist were hardly paleontologists, they did a credible job with their layman knowledge of zoology and prehistoric life, creating a tactile sense of time, place, and reality that was innovative. These were situations readers young and old could relate to on a primal level no narrative medium had previously tapped: and comics were the ideal medium for such stories. As demonstrated in even the finest "paleo" short stories and novels, from 1934's *Before the Dawn* by mathematician Eric Temple Bell (writing as John Taine) to paleontologist Robert Bakker's recent *Raptor Red*, the written word alone does not lend itself to "pure" dinosaur fiction. Those damned Latin species names stop a reader's eye dead, and the repetition of either species names or personalized monikers or nicknames become intrusive; further, the contemporary vernacular of even the most careful author wrenches us out of the primordial narrative. In comics, however, we see the creatures, identify and distinguish them by sight, and know with a glance their diets, strengths, and vulnerabilities. Identifying markings, patterns, or coloration allow both artist and reader to individualize the creatures themselves in a way that is difficult at best via text alone, and the body language of the drawn creatures invites a primal bond between reader and animal almost impossible to evoke with such urgency in literature. Comics, as a medium, is perfectly suited to this idiosyncratic genre, and the appeal of dinosaurs to the traditional comics readership is universal.

Turok's editor was so sure this creative team was on to something that the splash panel of "The Plight of the Plesiosaur" labeled this self-contained parable as the maiden voyage of a new series, entitled "Young Earth." And so began a comics series that appeared in almost every issue of *Turok, Son of Stone* for well over a decade. "Young Earth" was a revelation: the first true dinosaur comic book series, focusing solely on the prehistoric animals (and, later, on prehistoric man) in compact, concise narratives. Newman's scripts were marvelously evocative and concise; Maxon's sketchy, energetic art enlivened the series for the duration of *Turok's* run. Though the birth of this series, and its impressive longevity, seemed (and remains) inconsequential to those who chart the ebb and flow of comics history and pop culture, it was significant, anticipating all that was to come, including Delgado's *Age of Reptiles*, my own *Tyrant*, and the book you now hold in your hands.

IV.

The next significant landmark dinosaur comic emerged in 1959 from a rather unlikely source; and it becomes, somewhat, part of my own story. For two decades, Gilberton Publications had built their publishing empire entirely upon comic book adaptations of classic literature: the venerable and celebrated *Classics Illustrated* series. By the late 1950's, Gilbert on had diversified, enhancing its line with the fairy-tale fueled *Classics Illustrated Junior* adaptations, and the encyclopedic *The World Around Us* which offered "A World of Adventure, Travel & History" to more studious comic book readers. This monthly educational series offered 72-page square-bound overviews on a variety of subjects, from military histories (*The Illustrated Story of the Marines; The Coast Guard;* etc.) and animals (*The Illustrated Story of Horses; Dogs;* etc.) to more esoteric fare (*The Illustrated Story of Pirates; Ghosts; Magic;* etc.).

I was four years old when the cover of the November 1959 issue of *The World Around Us* #15 leaped off the comic book racks at Towne's Market in Essex Junction, Vermont. Beneath the bright yellow masthead *The Illustrated Story*

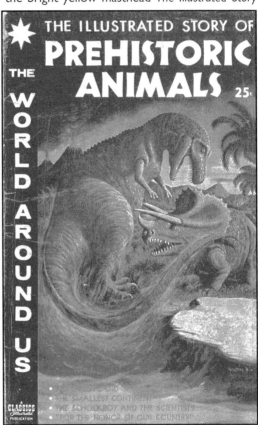

The Illustrated Story Of Prehistoric Animals - Nov. 1959, World-Wide Publications Inc.

of *Prehistoric Animals* was a vivid painting of a Tyrannosaurus rex and a Triceratops locked in mortal combat as twin volcanoes erupted in the background. It was the first comic I recall wanting; my mother obliged, and my life forever changed. This new artifact was a thing of beauty to me (and, in hindsight, it still is). Dinosaur children's books had been a fixture of my existence, but this was something new, and somehow more vital, more alive, than the most beloved of all my dino books. I poured over its pages, brooded over its single most glaring error (the coelacanth in the very first story, "The Fish That Never Died," was erroneously drawn as an icthyosaur), labored over my own crude copies of the art in my favorite panels, read and reread the comic (as best as I could read at age four). I wore out my first copy so quickly that my mother still had time to buy a replacement copy off the newsstand. I was sorely disappointed when the next issue of *The World Around Us* wasn't dedicated to more prehistoric material -- it was instead *The Illustrated Story of the Crusades* -- leaving me to make due with *Turok*, as usual. Though written and rendered for the most part

6

in the staid mode of most Gilberton titles, and lacking the immediacy and electricity of the *Turok* "Young Earth" series, *The Illustrated Story of Prehistoric Animals* formalized and legitimized the dinosaur comic. However restraining the Gilberton editorial templates, among the artists illustrating the dry-as-chalk-dust narratives were masters like Al Williamson, George Evans, Reed Crandall, and Sam Glanzman. Al Williamson

THE DIPLODOCUS * WAS LONGER AND SLIMMER THAN THE BRONTOSAURUS. HE WAS EIGHTY-FIVE FEET LONG AND SIXTEEN FEET HIGH. HIS NOSE WAS ON TOP OF HIS HEAD SO HE COULD PUT HIS FACE UNDER WATER TO FIND MARSHY PLANTS TO EAT.

* Dip-lah-do-cus

Sam Glanzman Art - From "Giants In The Earth" in *The World Around Us #15, The Illustrated Story Of Prehistoric Animals*, Nov. 1959, Gilberton World-Wide Publications, Inc.

and George Evan's rendition of "Death of the Dinosaur" seemed positively lush and grandiose -- almost operatic -- in its mournful undertone of irrevocable loss: the final panel of dinosaur life, as paired Trachodons and Triceratops move toward a distant river, haunted me like no other comic panel ever had. But most mesmerizing of all were Sam Glanzman's pages, illustrating the eight-page "Giants in the Earth." Though there was little sequential intensity to the piece -- composed, essentially, of unconnected single-page splashes depicting the "star" dinosaurs circa 1959 pop science, many of which were clearly drawn from Charles Knight's paintings – it was Glanzman's drawing and inking style

that I found riveting. Glanzman dared to be "messy." His jungles and saurians were fly-blown and gritty, stray drops of water, slaver, and shreds of vegetation dropped away from his dinosaurs, unidentifiable bits of matter spun or hung in the air, as if suspended or moved by the heat and humidity. I'd been around enough barnyards, ponds, and forests to know nature was as "messy" as Glanzman's tableaus. Glanzman eschewed the neat sterility of most natural history and paleontology art, and seemed more tactile, more alive, than any art I'd ever laid eyes on before. His mere eight pages of comic art blew away every recreation of dinosaur life I'd ever seen before. I was hooked. From that day on, I had a Tyrannosaur on my back. I was a dinosaur comic junkie in need of a fix – of which there were precious few.

Almost three years later, in 1962, Gilberton and *Classics Illustrated* obliged with a giant "Special Issue," *Prehistoric World*. Though it was a fine comic indeed, featuring at least one innovative bit of sequential experimentation (the three-page "The Wonderful Earth Movie," presenting tiny panels illustrating an imaginary one-year-long movie about the history of life on Earth, offering a humbling, mind-boggling perspective on how fleeting man's cameo in that history is) and plenty of dinosaurs, it didn't have anything approaching those pages by Sam Glanzman, and thus never assumed the mythic stature of that first *Classics Illustrated* dinosaur comic.

So desperate was my hunger, and unproductive my search, that even a Catholic comic book might offer sanctuary. Among the treasures of my youth I ache to hold again in my hands again is a one-off issue of the Catholic comic book series *Treasure Chest*, which for one glorious issue in the late 1950's or very early 1960's featured a cover story on dinosaurs. It was, if memory serves, as much an educational dinosaur comic as the *Classics Illustrated* specials.
A more contemporary Christian (and stridently anti-Catholic) comic book approach to the subject can be found in Jack T. Chick's notorious religious tracts, where the controversy over evolution is tackled time and time again -- most memorably in Chick's mini-comic anti-evolution screed *Big Daddy*, and most gloriously in The Crusaders' color comic book *Primal Man?* The fossil record of early man commands more attention and takes more heat than the dinosaurs do in these comics, but *Primal Man?*

plays the faux-fossil card of the Texan Paluxy river bed dinosaur footprints which appear alongside (carved) human prints, a favorite Creationist strategy.

V.

As "Young Earth" continued in every issue of *Turok*, competing publishers jumped on the monster-boom bandwagon of the early 1960's, spicing their giant monster comics with the occasional back-up strip dedicated to prehistoric animals and early man. None of these approached the quality of either "Young Earth" or the *Classics Illustrated* comics. Dell's own mercurial *Kona, Monarch of Monster Isle* (debuting early in 1962) was drawn by Sam Glanzman and brimmed with imaginative renditions of dinosaurs, mutants, and monsters, but only its second issue featured a perfunctory one-pager dedicated to dinosaurs.

Furthermore, editorial standards at publishers varied: Charlton Comics were much less exacting than those at Dell, Gold Key, or Gilberton. Proper spelling (much less any semblance of scientific accuracy) was a struggle on the best of days. Among the misspellings we young comic-reading punks particularly prized

MALE AND FEMALE, THESE HUGE CREATURES, MATES! TINY BRAINS, HUGE BODIES, THEY LIVED BY NERVE REFLEXES RATHER THAN MIND! BUT THEY WERE YOUNG AND IN THEIR PRIME...

Artist Unknown - From "From Beyond Time" in Gorgo #13, Jun. 1963, Charlton Comics.

was "Vistit to Earth" in *Gorgo #23*. Thus, at the age of ten, "vistit" entered our vocabulary as a synonym for "breast," a term that was vague and disorienting enough to be spoken aloud in the vicinity of adults without provoking a slap to the head.

The prehistoric back-up comics in the pages of Charlton's *Gorgo* and *Konga* comics were, and remain, laughable curios, of interest primarily for their art -- or their risible crudity, which

invited derisive snorts from kids and outright laughter from older readers. Much as I loved Steve Ditko and the Montes/Bache art in both titles, there was no mistaking the abysmal (and always uncredited) rush-jobs most of the back-up pieces truly were, from *Gorgo #3's* slap dash "Men and Monsters" onwards. However rough and ready the art might have been in Ditko's rare appearance among these back-up strips , there was no mistaking his work: it was

THE RULERS

THIS IS A STORY OF EARTH... OF THIS PLANET. THIS IS THE STORY OF THE RULERS OF EARTH. EARTH IS A GLOBE IN A GALAXY THAT HAS AS ITS CORE THE FIERY SUN, AND ON EARTH AS THE EON SEASONS PASS, SPECIES RULE THE SURFACE, RULE THE PLANET! THIS IS THEIR STORY.

Steve Ditko Art - From *Konga #3, 1961, Charlton Comics.*

alive and invigorating, even at its silliest (e.g., a caveman smashing out the teeth of an attacking saber-tooth cat in a cartoonish gag in "Why He Survived" in *Konga #8*). The rest of the back-up stories seemed anonymous and disturbingly amateurish; our first intimations, really, that mere mortals were responsible for the comics we devoured.

The complete lack of research evident in a strip like "The Beginning" in 1963's *Reptisaurus Special Edition #1* yielded delirious creatures unlike any that ever lived -- including bizarre putty-like fishes with fleshy, eyeless faces and a cross between a unicorn and a dragon that was supposed to represent the first mammals -- and the featureless phallic Brontosaur of "The Victor" from *Konga #19*. The stiff, stodgy art for "From Beyond Time" in *Gorgo #13* seemed to imply that Brontosaurs (the outmoded moniker for Apatosaurus) mated by rubbing their necks together ("...but they were young and in their prime..."), provoking some sniggering on the playground at the close of that school year (it could also be argued that the latter piece also fueled my own dinosaur comics, as a classmate then told me – at the age of eight – "Jeez, Bissette, you draw better dinosaur comics than this!"). Like I said, it was slim pickings for a dinosaur-comic junkie. I made due with the rock-solid *Turok*, the hallucinogenic *Kona*, and the lunatic

Robert Kanigher scripted, Andru/Esposito-illustrated "The War That Time Forgot!" in *Star-Spangled War Stories*, and dreamed about drawing my own honest-to-God dinosaur comics one day. As time demonstrated, I was hardly alone.

VI

The "science comic" format was revamped completely by Harvard graduate and underground cartoonist Larry Gonick's inspired *The Cartoon History of the Universe* (launched in 1978, from Rip Off Press). The irreverent first volume, "The

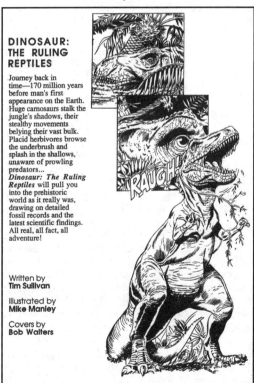

Larry Gonick Art - From The Cartoon History Of The Universe, Volume 1: the evolution of everything, 1978. Rip Off Press, Inc.

Evolution of Everything (including Sex!!)" set the tone for Gonick's highly-entertaining, highly-informative approach to a once-static form, and dinosaurs figured prominently in that debut issue. Fellow underground cartoonist Greg Irons raised the bar around the same time with his trio of coloring books for Bellerophon Press, particularly *All New Dinosaurs and Their Friends* and *The Last of the Dinosaurs*, which incorporated radical revisionist thought and new discoveries in the science of paleontology.

These discoveries trickled into the pop culture, aided (and in part spearheaded) by a new generation of paleo artists. Prominent among was William Stout, whose book *The Dinosaurs: A Fantastic New View of A Lost Era* (with text by William Service; Byron Preiss/Bantam/Mallard,

1981) set a new high-water mark for the field. Stout's showcase of exquisite dinosaur portraits and tableaus reached a much wider audience, inspiring a new wave of budding cartoonists. Still, my own experience in the comics field (since 1976) proved that editors and publishers were reluctant to indulge a "pure" dinosaur comic: super heroes, time travel fantasies, "lost worlds," and city-stomping resurrected saurians still held sway.

That all changed in the 1990's, as the growing popularity of pop science and science fiction books, magazines, TV shows, and movies featuring dinosaurs gained critical mass. You could smell the blood in the air: the pop-cultural cycle had turned anew. Dinosaurs were "in" and those of us who grew up aching to draw our own dinosaur comics could wait no longer. The wave swelled to tsunami proportions with the publication of Michael Crichton's novel *Jurassic Park*.

In 1989, Dark Horse Comics announced *Dinosaur: The Ruling Reptiles* from writer Tim Sullivan and artist Mike Manley; alas, it was not to be,

Bob Walters, Mike Manley Art - From Dark Horse Futures '89, 1989, Dark Horse Comics, Inc.

supplanted five years later by Ricardo Delgado's delirious, phantasmagoric full-color *Age of Reptiles*, a text-less narrative brimming with movement, action, and (of course) dinosaurs. Delgado's mini-series proved successful enough to spawn an even more expansive sequel, *Age of Reptiles: The*

Hunt. In the meantime, other publishers mounted their own dinosaur comics. Under their imprint "Tome Press," Caliber Press released the two-issue *Dinosaurs: An Illustrated Guide* by Charles Yates, an unsophisticated variant composed of single-page and panel snapshots of various prehistoric species accompanied by captions of descriptive text, peppered with occasional pages of non-sequitor sequential action. More ambitious (and better financed) was Marvel Comics' Epic Comics' 1992 mini-series *Dinosaurs: A Celebration,* conceived and helmed by editor Steve White as a collective of self-standing comic narratives by a variety of writers and artists, grounded in the most current paleontological science available. For my own part, I completed work on the first

Stephen R. Bissette Art - *From S.R. Bissette's Tyrant #3, Jan. 1995. SpiderBaby Graphics and Publications.*

issue of *Tyrant*, and debuted the short-lived self-published venture in 1994. These descendants of Newman and Maxon's "Young Earth" bred and fled quickly; as the comics industry implosion of the late 1990's rocked the field, only the fittest survived.

Among the hale and hearty survivors intent on carrying on was Jim Lawson, whose concept for *Paleo* was already taking shape. Mirage Studios published Jim's science fiction adventure mini-series *Dino Island* in 1993. Shortly afterwards, Jim began work in earnest on his own "pure" dinosaur comic, *Paleo.*

About which, I need not say much more. All you really need to know is in the pages that follow. All you really need to do is read them, and let Jim take you through the doorway he has forged into our shared prehistoric dreams, reveries, and fantasies. Notice the fully-realized environments, the rich sense of lives lived beyond the border of mere comic panels and pages. What you may not notice is how personal this body of work is to Jim. Maybe I'm too familiar with Jim's immediate circle, but it seems to me there are clear correlations between the struggles his antediluvian protagonists endure and what I know of Jim's experiences. The arenas are very different, the obstacles more lethal, the armor tougher, the teeth sharper, but Jim has, in his own way, walked in their footsteps.

I'm happy to report that Jim is still working on new *Paleo* material. So after you enjoy this collection -- which I suspect many young readers will pour over

time and time again, wearing it out as thoroughly as I wore out my first copy of *The Illustrated Story of Prehistoric Animals* — rest assured, there will be more. Given the incredible volume of pages Jim has created over the past fifteen years for other comics and projects, I don't think it's either unreasonable or premature to hope that Jim might match or break Rex Maxon's "Young Earth" record. For now, though, this book is plenty. Enjoy.

Stephen R. Bissette
July 2003
Vermont

(Special thanks from Steve Bissette to Sam Kujava for the 11th hour research assist.)

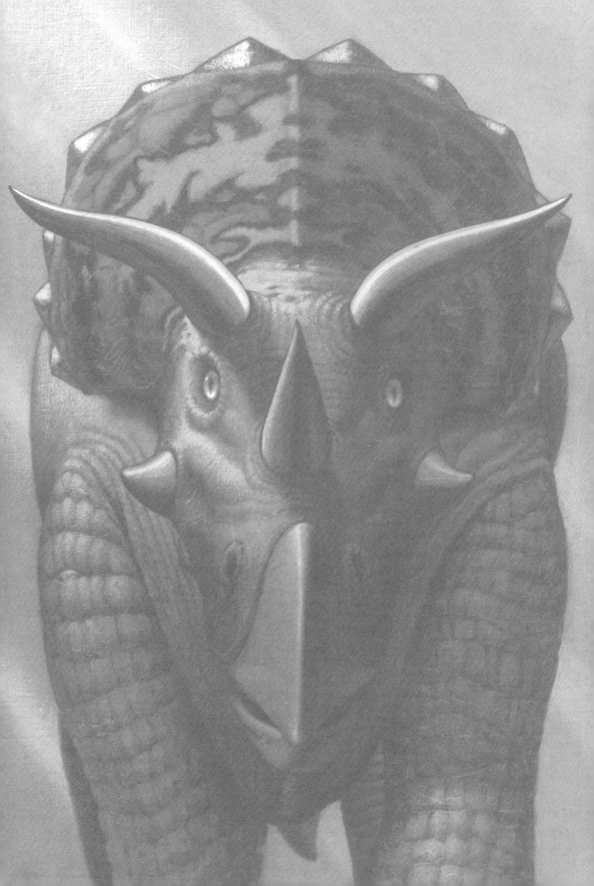

Book One

NO MATTER HOW LARGE OR HOW
POWERFUL, THERE'S ALWAYS
ANOTHER WHO IS BIGGER AND
STRONGER. THE FATE OF EVEN
THE MOST FEARSOME AND
TERRIBLE DINOSAUR RESTED NOT
ALWAYS ON SHEER POWER BUT
OFTEN ON SHEER LUCK...

JIM
LAW
SON

A JUVENILE TRICERATOPS FEMALE FEEDS *CONTENTEDLY* AT THE FOREST'S EDGE...

... IT'S EASY TO *FORGET* THE DAYS SPENT HUDDLING TOGETHER, WAITING FOR THE RAIN TO *STOP.*

NOW THERE'S *MORE* THAN ENOUGH...

... FOR *EVERYONE.*

3

SUDDENLY, THE SMALL MAMMALS SCATTER...

BEHIND THE YOUNG TRICERATOPS, A *NOISE*... A SOFT BRUSHING OF BRANCHES...

SHE TURNS TO JOIN THE HERD...

SEEING THE *DASPLETOSAURS*, SHE *FREEZES*...

THEIR SMELL *FILLS* HER NOSTRILS...

HER MIND GOES *WHITE*...

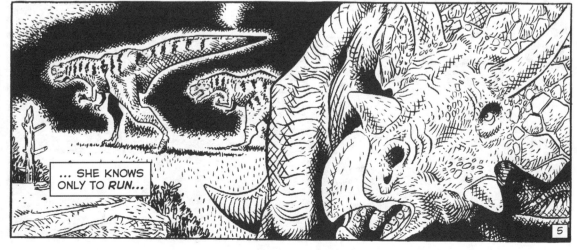

... SHE KNOWS ONLY TO *RUN*...

...AS FAR AS SHE CAN...

...AS FAST AS SHE CAN...

CRUNCHK!

7

SHE IS *STARTLED* WHEN THE FOREST BEGINS TO *MOVE.*

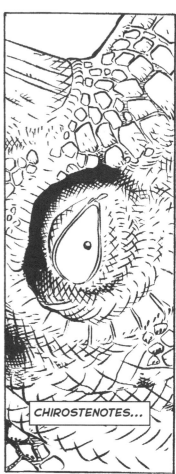

CHIROSTENOTES...

... TINY *PREDATORS*, NO BIGGER THAN ONE OF HER FEET, THEY SPEND THEIR LIVES IN THE *UNDERGROWTH,* HUNTING TINY MAMMALS AND INSECTS.

SHE RUNS, *BUCKING* AND *SLASHING* AT THE FOREST...

...NOT ALLOWING IT THE *OPPORTUNITY* TO *RECAPTURE* HER.

THE FOREST RELINQUISHES...

...ALLOWING IN *LIGHT* AND THE *SMELL* OF *DUST* AND *GRASS*.

15

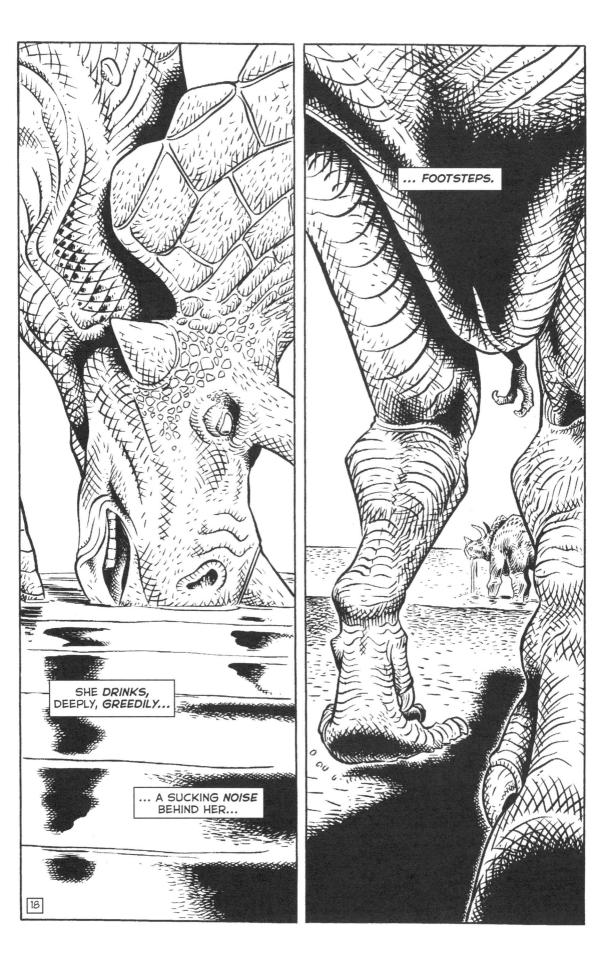

... FOOTSTEPS.

SHE *DRINKS*, DEEPLY, *GREEDILY*...

... A SUCKING *NOISE* BEHIND HER...

18

SHE *KNOWS* THAT SHE MUST AVOID *STOPPING* DIRECTLY IN *FRONT* OF THE CARNIVORE...

...FOR ITS *LEGS* ARE *POORLY* DESIGNED FOR *TWISTING*, AND THIS WAY SHE CAN KEEP HIM *OFF BALANCE.*

HE TAKES A STEP BACK, *ADJUSTING* TO FACE HER... THEIR EYES ARE *LOCKED*...

... EACH WAITING FOR A *MISSTEP*...

...*A MISTAKE.*

IT HAPPENS SO *QUICKLY...*

A HUGE *DEINOSUCHUS* *EXPLODES* FROM THE WATER...

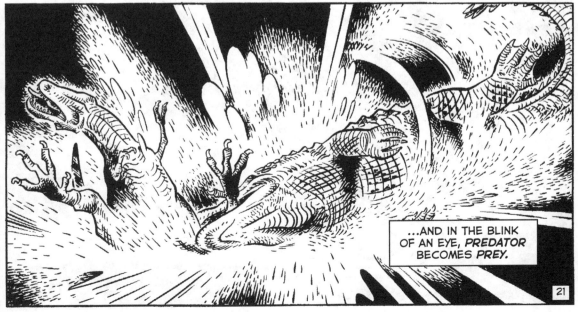

...AND IN THE BLINK OF AN EYE, *PREDATOR* BECOMES *PREY.*

THE DASPLETOSAUR *SQUEALS* IN *PAIN*...

...IT DOESN'T LAST *LONG*.

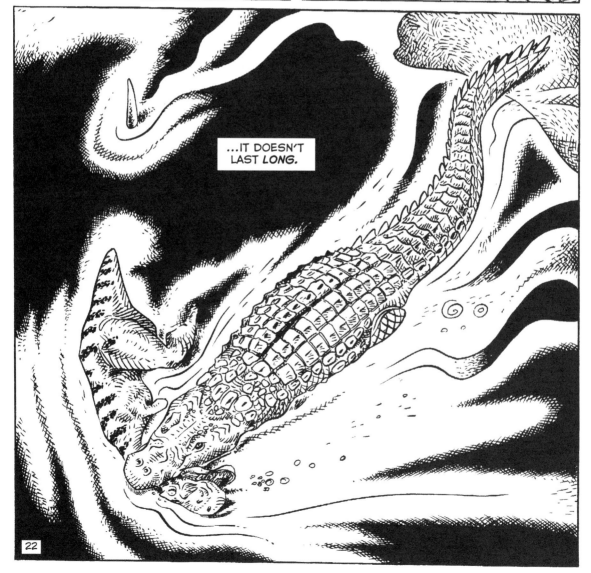

22

SHE *CAN'T* KNOW *GRATITUDE,* OR APPRECIATE HER *GOOD LUCK*...

...THE *DEINOSUCHUS* COULD HAVE JUST AS EASILY TAKEN *HER.*

THE BREEZE CARRIES A *FAMILIAR* SCENT...

...THE YOUNG TRICERATOPS BELLOWS A *GREETING*...

23

...SHE IS *HOME* ONCE MORE.

Book Two

SOMETIMES WE ALL NEED TO KNOW WHEN TO GIVE IN...

IT COMES *SWIFTLY* AND WITHOUT *WARNING...*

...HE HARDLY HAS TIME TO BRACE HIMSELF FOR THE *ATTACK.*

1

ALTHOUGH *BARELY* MORE THAN *ONE HUNDRED POUNDS*, THE WEIGHT OF THE ALPHA'S BODY KNOCKS THE YOUNG *DROMEOSAUR* ONTO HIS BACK.

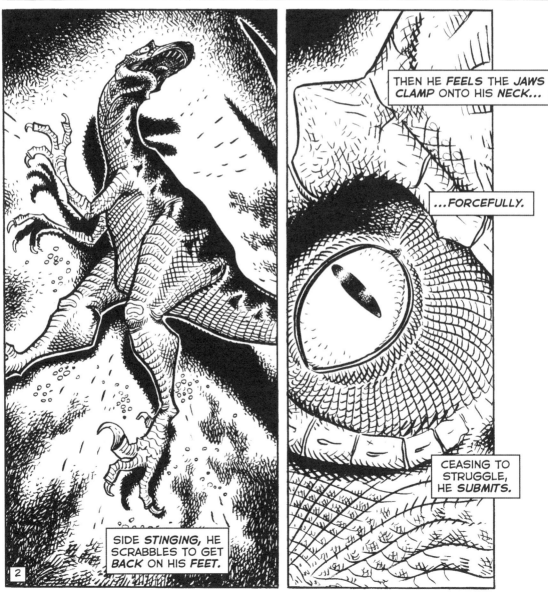

THEN HE *FEELS* THE *JAWS CLAMP* ONTO HIS *NECK...*

...FORCEFULLY.

CEASING TO STRUGGLE, HE *SUBMITS.*

SIDE *STINGING*, HE SCRABBLES TO GET *BACK* ON HIS *FEET.*

2

THE *DISPLAY* IS *OVER.*

THE REST OF THE PACK *STARE* INQUISITIVELY, THE THREE *FEMALES* CHIRPING *EXCITEDLY* AMONG THEMSELVES.

SNIFFING THE AIR, THE ALPHA MALE *TROTS* AWAY, AND THE PACK *FOLLOWS* OBEDIENTLY.

THE YOUNG MALE DROMEOSAUR *RISES,* CAREFULLY *AVOIDING* THE *GAZES* OF THE TWO OTHER *ADOLESCENT MALES.*

3

THEY *TRAVEL* IN *SINGLE FILE...* THIS IS SO, WHEN THEY *APPROACH* THEIR *QUARRY*, THEY APPEAR AS A *SINGLE INDIVIDUAL*.

SOON THEY COME ACROSS A FEMALE *EUOPLOCEPHALUS* WITH HER YOUNG.

AS THEY APPROACH, THE ALPHA MALE *CLICKS* OUT A *SIGNAL* AND THE PACK SPREADS OUT, *ENCIRCLING* THE *ANKYLOSAURIDS*.

THE EUOCEPHALUS ASSUMES A *DEFENSIVE POSTURE* AS HER TWO YOUNG *CROUCH* DOWN ON THE GROUND BENEATH HER.

THE PACK *HESITATES,* LOOKING TO SOMEHOW *DRAW* THE MOTHER *AWAY* FROM HER *YOUNG.*

HOWEVER, SHE IS *UNWILLING* TO MOVE, AND AT *TWENTY FEET LONG* AND *HEAVILY ARMORED,* SHE IS *MORE* THAN A *MATCH* FOR THE RELATIVELY *SMALL,* LITHE CARNIVORES.

FRUSTRATED, THE DROMEOSAURS *MOVE OFF.*

5

IT'S NOT *LONG* BEFORE THE ALPHA MALE ATTEMPTS TO *REASSERT* HIMSELF...

... THIS TIME HE PICKS ONE OF THE *FEMALES.*

SHE *BARKS* A WARNING, BUT MAKES NO ATTEMPT TO *REBUFF* HIS *AGGRESSIVENESS.*

HE TAKES HER *HEAD* IN HIS *JAWS* UNTIL SHE *SQUATS,* GIVING IN.

THE YOUNG MALE DROMEOSAUR HAS *NO* INTEREST IN THIS DISPLAY AND TURNS TOWARD THE *STREAM.*

A QUICK *NOISE* AND *MOVEMENT* CATCHES HIS ATTENTION.

7

PREY...

8

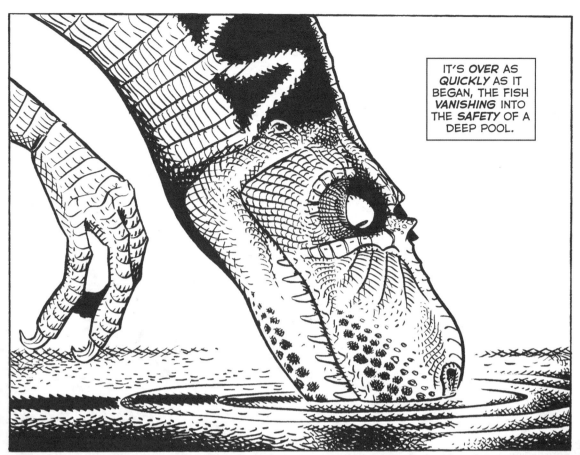

IT'S *OVER* AS *QUICKLY* AS IT BEGAN, THE FISH *VANISHING* INTO THE *SAFETY* OF A DEEP POOL.

THE DROMEOSAUR STANDS THERE *DUMBLY* FOR A MOMENT.

HE *STRAIGHTENS* UP, *SCANNING* THE FOREST AROUND HIM FOR HIS *MISSING* QUARRY.

DOWNSTREAM, A HERD OF *TSINTAOSAURS* SLOWLY *SHUFFLES* AWAY. THE *LARGER MALES* TAKE NOTICE OF THE SMALL THEROPOD AND, DESPITE FEELING NO DIRECT *THREAT,* URGE THE OTHERS TO *MOVE AWAY* WITH THEIR LOW, DULL GRUNTS.

AS IF SUDDENLY *NOTICING* THE PRESENCE OF THE SMALL PREDATOR, THE TSINTAOSAURUS *SWINGS* AROUND TO *FACE* HIM.

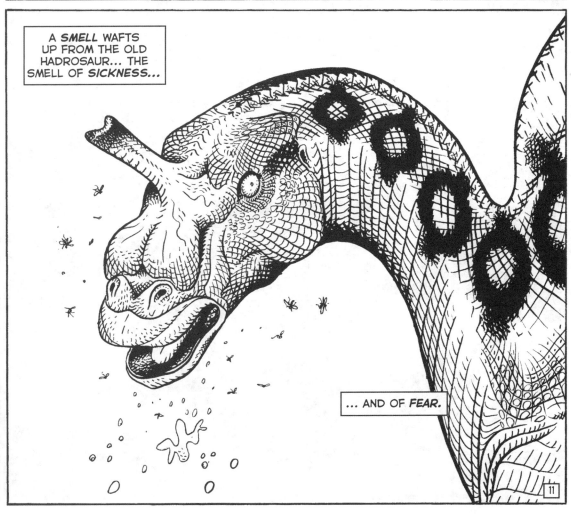

A *SMELL* WAFTS UP FROM THE OLD HADROSAUR... THE SMELL OF *SICKNESS*...

... AND OF *FEAR.*

11

THE OTHERS *ARRIVE*, AND THE YOUNG DROMEOSAUR *BOWS* HIS *HEAD* AS THE ALPHA MALE STRIDES BY, *BARKING* AND *CLICKING* FOR THE PACK TO *SPREAD OUT.*

THE OLD TSINTAOSAUR *SHUFFLES* AROUND, IN AN ATTEMPT TO GET ITSELF INTO A *DEFENSIVE* POSITION.

ITS *MOVEMENTS* ARE SLOW, *JERKY.* IT SEEMS UNABLE TO *FOCUS* THROUGH ITS DULL, *GLAZED* EYES.

A *NIP* AT ITS *BACK LEG* IS ALL IT TAKES TO THROW THE OLD ONE OFF *BALANCE.* IT SWINGS ITS TAIL *CLUMSILY.*

IT *STUMBLES...*

THE ALPHA MALE STANDS *ATOP* THE *KILL*, BARKING AND *GLOATING*.

THE OTHERS MILL AROUND *IMPATIENTLY*, WAITING FOR THE *SIGNAL* THAT IT IS ALRIGHT FOR THEM TO *FEED*.

THEY CLICK THEIR CLAWS IN *ANTICIPATION*.

THE YOUNG MALE *SCANS* UP AND DOWN THE *STREAM*.

IT IS *NOT* OVER.

15

THEY MUST REMAIN *VIGILANT...*

... DOWNED *PREY* IS AN INVITATION TO *OPPORTUNISTIC* PREDATORS.

IT DOESN'T TAKE *LONG.*

SEVEN HEADS *TURN* IN *UNISON*, ACKNOWLEDGING THE *SOUND* COMING UP THE STREAM.

IT IS AN *ALBERTOSAUR*.

17

THE KILL *MUST* BE *DEFENDED.*

THE ALPHA MALE BARKS OUT *WARNINGS* AS THE PACK FORMS A LINE *BETWEEN* THE INTRUDER AND THE *CARCASS.*

18

PROBABLY FORCED *OUT* OF ITS HERD AS IT DREW CLOSE TO *MATING AGE*, THIS YOUNG MALE HAS HAD TO FEND FOR ITSELF.

ITS HUNGER HAS MADE IT *RECKLESS...*

20

THE SHEER **FORCE** OF THE **LARGER ANIMAL'S** CHARGE BOWLS OVER THE YOUNG DROMEOSAUR...

... AND **ATOP** HIS **PRIZE,** THE ALPHA MALE CONTINUES TO BARK, **REFUSING** TO **SUBMIT...**

... AND IN THE ALBERTOSAUR'S **MOUTH,** OVER THE **SOUND** OF **SNAPPING** BONES, THE YOUNG DROMEOSAUR THINKS HE **STILL** HEARS THE **BARKING.**

21

THE ALBERTOSAUR PICKS UP THE *CARCASS* AND *DRAGS* IT OFF...

THE PACK WATCHES *DUMBLY*... THEIR LEADER IS *GONE*...

THE FEMALES *CHITTER* LOWLY AMONGST THEMSELVES...

...IT IS AN *UNSURE* NOISE.

THE PACK MUST HAVE A *LEADER*...

...OR IT WILL NOT *SURVIVE*.

23

24

RELEASING HIS RIVAL, THE YOUNG MALE DROM STANDS UP *PROUDLY.*

HE TURNS TO *VIEW* THE FEMALES, STANDING IN A GROUP, *WATCHING* INTENTLY.

EMBOLDENED, HE STRIDES UP TO THEM AND *GRABS* THE CLOSEST ONE'S *HEAD* IN HIS *JAWS*...

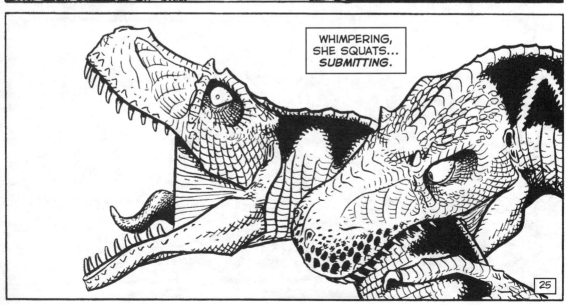

WHIMPERING, SHE SQUATS... *SUBMITTING.*

25

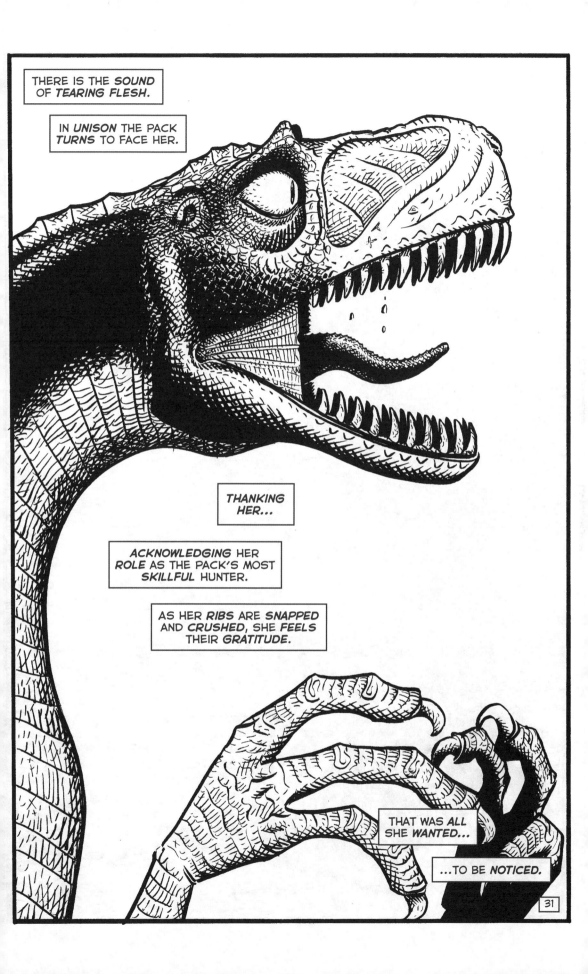

32

THE
END

Book Three

A SEEMINGLY CRUEL, SAVAGE WORLD, NO SYMPATHY OR REMORSE FOR THE WEAK... SAD IT'S TRUE. IT IS THE WAY OF THE WILD.

THE YOUNG **STEGOCERAS** RISES **SLOWLY**, STRETCHING TO RELIEVE THE **STIFFNESS** IN HIS **LEGS**.

AT **FOUR MONTHS OLD**, HE AND HIS TWO **SISTERS** ARE ALREADY **ONE-THIRD** THE SIZE OF THEIR **MOTHER**.

YAWN

THEY ARE BIG ENOUGH TO **TRAVEL**.

NOW, AFTER WALKING FOR **SEVERAL** DAYS, THEY ARE NEARLY TO THE UPPER **MEADOWS** AND **FORESTS** OF WHAT WILL SOMEDAY BE KNOWN AS THE **JUDITH RIVER FORMATION** OF **ALBERTA, CANADA**.

IT IS A *BEAUTIFUL*, CLEAR DAY.

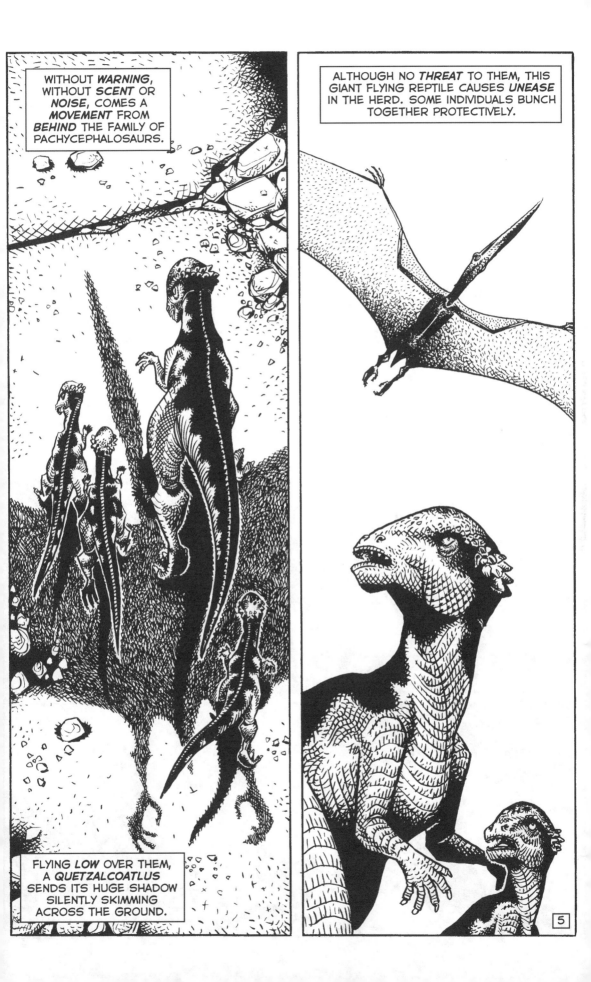

WITHOUT *WARNING*, WITHOUT *SCENT* OR *NOISE*, COMES A *MOVEMENT* FROM *BEHIND* THE FAMILY OF PACHYCEPHALOSAURS.

ALTHOUGH NO *THREAT* TO THEM, THIS GIANT FLYING REPTILE CAUSES *UNEASE* IN THE HERD. SOME INDIVIDUALS BUNCH TOGETHER PROTECTIVELY.

FLYING *LOW* OVER THEM, A *QUETZALCOATLUS* SENDS ITS HUGE SHADOW SILENTLY SKIMMING ACROSS THE GROUND.

5

THE LITTLE STEGOCERAS *STARES* INQUISITIVELY AS HIS SISTERS HUDDLE *CLOSE* TO THEIR MOTHER.

THE QUETZALCOATLUS IS *MAGNIFICENT* AND *STRANGE* TO THE YOUNG DINOSAUR... A HINT OF *FEAR* STIRS WITHIN HIM...

...BUT HE FEELS *SAFE* NEXT TO HIS *MOTHER.*

7

THE HERD HAS WALKED INTO A *TRAP!*

POWERFUL AND *DEADLY* AT A RUN, THE STEGOCERAS' *HEAD-BUTTING* ABILITY MAKES THEM *FORMIDABLE* PREY.

BUT *HERE* ON THIS *NARROW* MOUNTAINSIDE, THEY *LACK* THE ROOM TO *DEFEND* THEMSELVES.

ADDITIONALLY, THEIR *UPRIGHT* STANCE MAKES THEM SOMEWHAT *SLOW* AND *AWKWARD...*

IT IS AS IF THE *DROMEOSAURS KNOW* THIS. IF THEY CAN *SEPARATE* THE HERD OR *DRIVE* AN INDIVIDUAL *OVER* THE *CLIFF*, IT WILL MAKE THEIR TASK EVEN *EASIER...*

LYING *MOTIONLESS*
IN THE SCRUB PINE,
HE KNOWS TO *WAIT*...

HE STAYS *HIDDEN* A *LONG TIME*...

... WAITING FOR HIS MOTHER'S *BLEATS*, SIGNALLING THAT IT WAS *SAFE* FOR HIM TO *COME OUT*.

AT THE *EDGE* OF HIS *VISION*, A *FAMILIAR SHAPE*...

... IT IS THE LARGE *FLYING REPTILE* HE HAD LAST SEEN WITH HIS *MOTHER*.

SLOWLY, CAUTIOUSLY, THE STEGOCERAS *RISES* FROM HIS *HIDING PLACE*.

11

A *SHORT* DISTANCE AWAY, HE SEES THAT THE CREATURE HAS *JOINED* HIS *MOTHER*. HE THINKS IT *UNUSUAL* THAT SHE HAS ALLOWED IT TO COME *SO CLOSE*.

HE STEPS *OUT* INTO THE *OPEN* AND BLEATS *PLAINTIVELY*.

12

FOR THE *FIRST* TIME IN HIS *SHORT* LIFE, HIS MOTHER DOES *NOT* *ACKNOWLEDGE* HIM.

HER JAWS HANG *OPEN* GROTESQUELY, *REVEALING* A *CHEWED TONGUE.*

HER *EYE*, LOCKED OPEN, *REVEALS* THE EMPTINESS OF THIS *BODY*... THIS *COLD* PIECE OF *MEAT* ON *BONE*...

...*NOTHING MORE.*

13

THE *QUETZALCOATLUS*
REGARDS THE YOUNG
DINOSAUR *INDIFFERENTLY*,
THEN *CONTINUES* TO *FEED*.

FROM *BEHIND* THEM COMES A *CRUNCHING*, A CLICKING OF *CLAWS* ON *STONE*... THE DROMEOSAURS HAVE *RETURNED*.

REARING *UP* ON ITS SCRAWNY LEGS, THE HUGE FLYING CREATURE *TURNS* TO FACE THE *PREDATORS*.

...THEN *LEAVE.* THEY HAD *UNDERESTIMATED* THE *SIZE* AND *AGGRESSIVENESS* OF THIS CREATURE.

IN AN *AWKWARD, TWISTING* WALK, THE QUETZALCOATLUS *HOISTS* HIMSELF TO THE EDGE OF THE CLIFF...

... AND *LAUNCHES* HIMSELF OUT OVER THE *VALLEY.*

THE STEGOCERAS *WATCHES* AS THE HUGE FLIER *RISES* ON THE WARM EVENING *AIR CURRENTS...*

...AND RETURNS TO THE *SAFETY* OF HIS *PERCH* OVERLOOKING THE VALLEY.

SOMETHING *PULLS* THE STEGOCERAS *UPWARD...*

19

...AWAY FROM *EVERYTHING* HE'S *KNOWN.*

IT IS *DARK* BY THE TIME HE REACHES THE CREATURE'S *PERCH*, ITS MISSHAPEN SILHOUETTE BLOTTING OUT THE *STARS*.

IF THE THING IS *AWARE* OF THE YOUNG DINOSAUR'S *PRESENCE*, IT GIVES *NO SIGN*. KEEPING A SMALL DISTANCE, THE STEGOCERAS LIES DOWN AND *SLEEPS*.

20

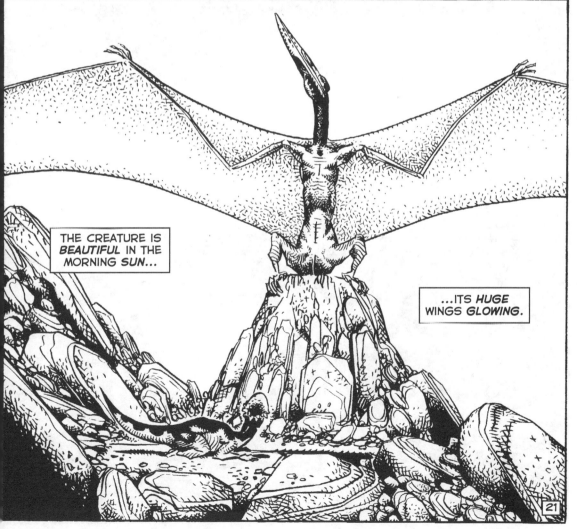

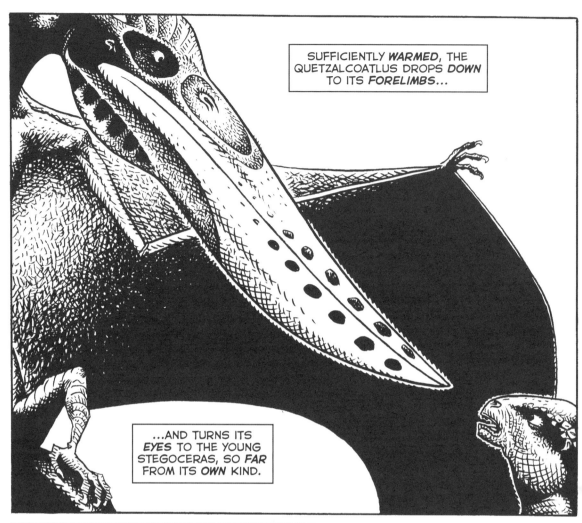

SUFFICIENTLY *WARMED*, THE QUETZALCOATLUS DROPS *DOWN* TO ITS *FORELIMBS*...

...AND TURNS ITS *EYES* TO THE YOUNG STEGOCERAS, SO *FAR* FROM ITS *OWN* KIND.

23

Book Four

A BUSY DAY IN THE LIFE
OF A PLOTOSAURUS.

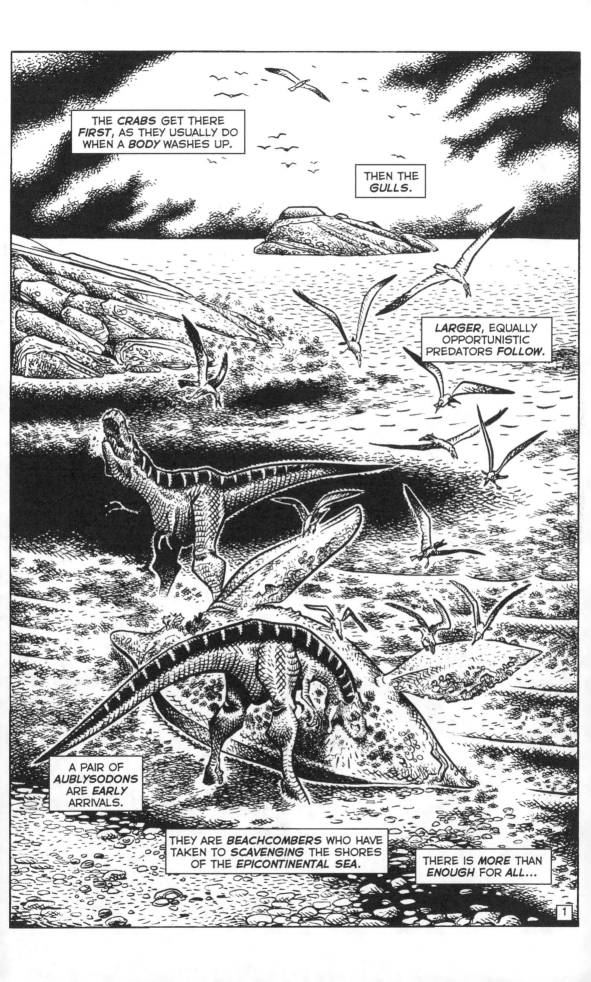

...FOR *NOW.*

THE *AUBLYSODONS* FEED *QUICKLY,* *GORGING* THEMSELVES.

THE SMALL *TYRANNOSAURIDS* KNOW THE *STENCH* OF THE CARCASS WILL SOON BRING *OTHERS.*

2

THEIR *PRIZE*...

... MUST BE *DEFENDED.*

3

6

THE *PLOTOSAURUS*, ALTHOUGH ONE OF THE MOST *POWERFUL* PREDATORS IN THE SEA, IS AT A *DISADVANTAGE* HERE.

THE CROCODILE, WITH ITS *WELL-DEVELOPED LEGS*, IS *SPEEDIER* AND MORE *MANEUVERABLE* IN THESE *SHALLOW* SHORELINE WATERS.

7

WITH THE *TASTE* OF ITS LOST PREY STILL *LINGERING* IN ITS *MOUTH*...

... THE PLOTOSAUR *RETREATS* TO THE *DEEP WATER.*

HE *HATED* GOING TO *LAND* -- THE CREATURES THERE *MOVED* IN *UNFAMILIAR* WAYS, AND HE FELT *AWKWARD* AND *VULNERABLE*...

...BUT THE *SCENT* OF THE *CARCASS* HAD BEEN *OVERWHELMING*.

BELOW HIM, SIX *DOLICHORYNCHOPS* STREAK BY -- THEY ARE A *SPEEDY*, VERY *LIMBER PLESIOSAUR* WITH A LONG NECK AND SLENDER JAWS.

ALTHOUGH THE *PLOTOSAURUS* IS ABLE TO *MATCH* THEM FOR *SPEED*, THE PLESIOSAURS' *MANEUVERABILITY* MAKES THEM *DIFFICULT PREY*.

STILL, OUT OF *CURIOSITY*, THE PLOTOSAURUS *TRAILS* THEM...

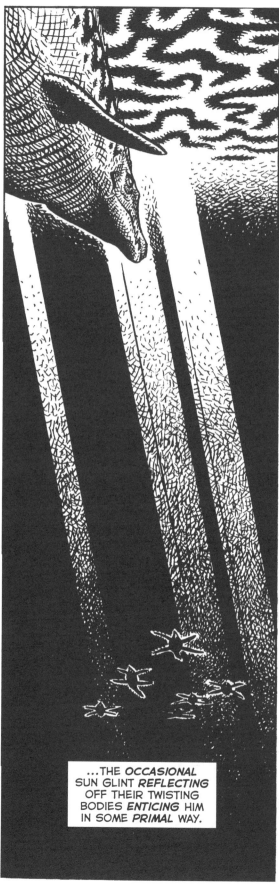

...THE *OCCASIONAL* SUN GLINT *REFLECTING* OFF THEIR TWISTING BODIES *ENTICING* HIM IN SOME *PRIMAL* WAY.

FROM OUT OF THE *DARKNESS*, THE SEA FLOOR *RISES* IN FRONT OF THE GREAT SEA REPTILE.

HE SWIMS ON *SLOWLY* NOW...

...THE *FILTER-FEEDING* ANIMALS, *ECHINODERMS*, WHICH CARPET THE SEA FLOOR GENTLY *RUB* HIS FLIPPERS AND BELLY.

11

UNABLE TO FOLLOW THE POLICHS ANY FURTHER...

... THE PLOTOSAURUS FLOATS, MOTIONLESS.

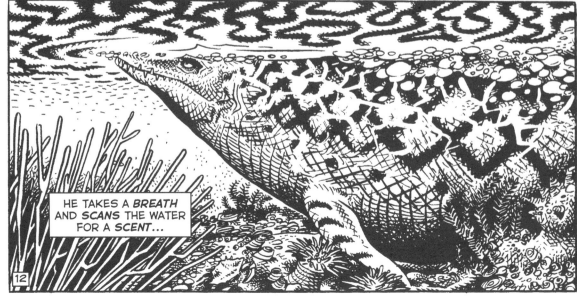

HE TAKES A BREATH AND SCANS THE WATER FOR A SCENT...

12

...ANY *VIBRATION*...

...THAT WOULD *LEAD* HIM TO *PREY.*

13

OFF IN THE *DISTANCE* FLOATS A GROUP OF *JELLYFISH.* IN THEIR MIDST SEVERAL *ARCHELON,* GIANT SEA TURTLES, *FEED.*

THEIR *MOVEMENTS* ARE *SLOW* AND *DELIBERATE,* UNLIKE THE MESSY, *VIOLENT* ATTACK OF THE *PLOTOSAURUS.*

14

HE IS *UNCOMFORTABLE* HERE...

... THE *SHALLOWNESS* OF THE *WATER* RESTRICTS HIS *MOVEMENTS* AND MAKES HIM *ILL AT EASE.*

WITH SEVERAL *VIOLENT TWISTS* OF HIS BODY, HE *SPEEDS* BACK TOWARD *DEEPER* WATER.

15

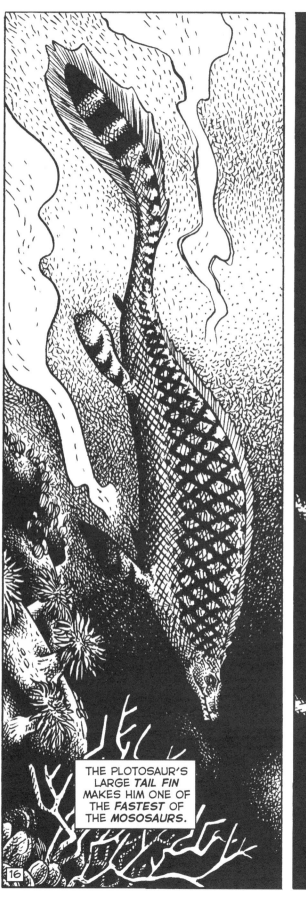

THE PLOTOSAUR'S LARGE *TAIL FIN* MAKES HIM ONE OF THE *FASTEST* OF THE *MOSOSAURS.*

16

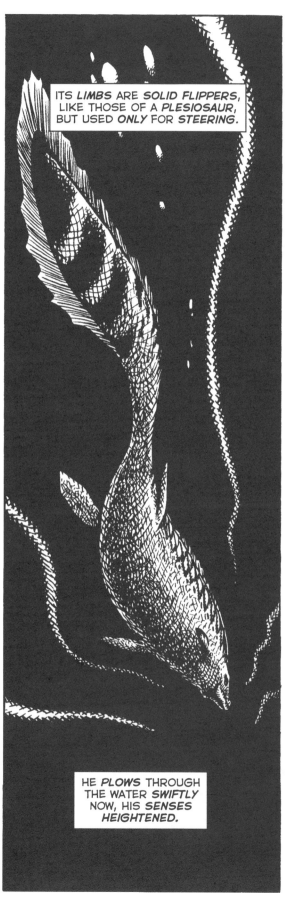

ITS *LIMBS* ARE *SOLID FLIPPERS,* LIKE THOSE OF A *PLESIOSAUR,* BUT USED *ONLY* FOR *STEERING.*

HE *PLOWS* THROUGH THE WATER *SWIFTLY* NOW, HIS *SENSES* HEIGHTENED.

THIS IS HIS FAVORITE *HUNTING TECHNIQUE*...

...TO COME UPON ITS *PREY* AND *STRIKE* UP OUT OF THE *DEPTHS*, TO CATCH HIS VICTIM *UNAWARE*... UNABLE TO *REACT*.

THERE IS *NOT* MUCH *NEED* FOR *CAUTION*...

...EXCEPT FOR *ANOTHER* MOSOSAUR, THERE IS *NOTHING* IN THE OCEAN TO *THREATEN* HIM.

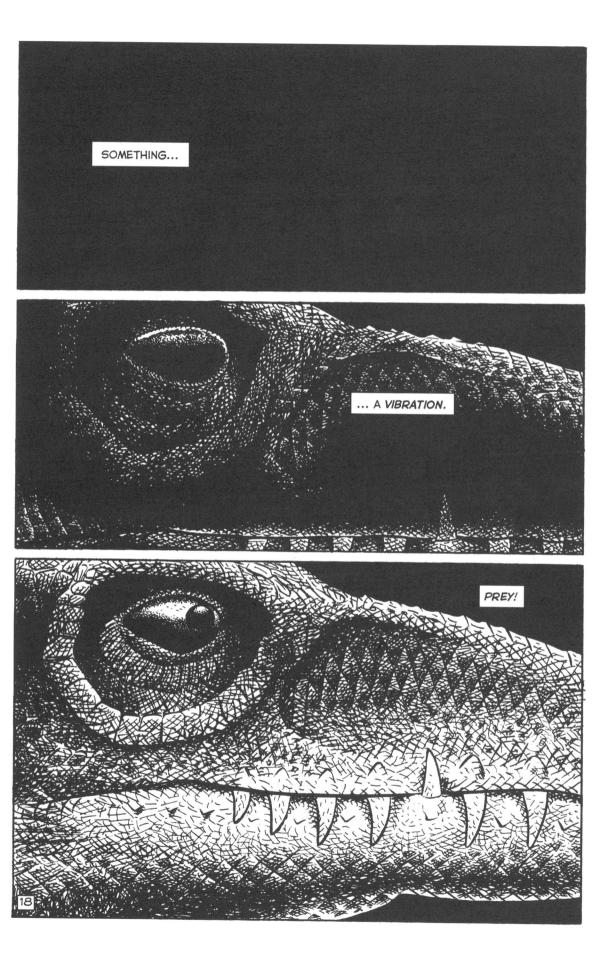

HIS *TEETH* NOW *SET,* HE *TWISTS...*

22

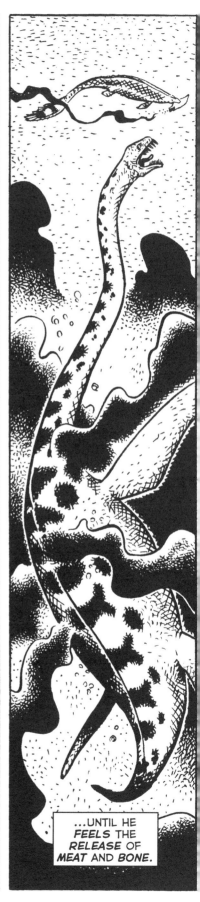

...UNTIL HE *FEELS* THE *RELEASE* OF *MEAT* AND *BONE.*

HE *WATCHES*...
AND *WAITS*...

...WAITS FOR THE *CREATURE* TO STOP *STRUGGLING*.

JERKING HIS *HEAD*, HE *SWALLOWS* THE FLIPPER *WHOLE*.

THE *RED OCEAN* GOES *STILL*.

23

Book Five

SELF INTEREST AND SELF PRESERVATION ARE PRIMARY INSTINCTS. ALL CREATURES WANT TO PROSPER AND ALL BELIEVE TO BE GUARANTEED ANOTHER SUNRISE. HOWEVER, THERE ARE NO GUARANTEES...

ESPECIALLY IN THE PALEOLITHIC WORLD.

THE *ATTACK* HAD BEEN *CLUMSY.*

HE *SHOULD* HAVE KNOWN *BETTER.*

1

HOWEVER, FOR WHAT THEY *LACKED* IN SPEED, NATURE *COMPENSATED* THEM WITH *ARMOR*...

HIS *PREFERRED* PREY HAD *ALWAYS* BEEN THE PLENTIFUL HERDS OF *HADROSAURS* THAT CALLED ALBERTA'S *RED DEER VALLEY* HOME.

BUT *LATELY*, THE *ALBERTOSAURUS* HAD NOTICED A *DECLINE* IN HIS ABILITY TO *PURSUE*.

HE WAS *FORCED* NOW TO SEEK OUT THE *SLOWER* BEASTS.

...AND *SPIKES*.

TO SUFFER A *WOUND* LIKE THIS WAS *SERIOUS* TO A *LARGE THEROPOD.*

INABILITY TO *HUNT* MEANT *STARVATION* AND *DEATH.*

THE *STYRACOSAURS,* HUFFING *DEFENSIVELY,* MOVED *SLOWLY* AWAY. THEY *KNEW* THE OLD, *WOUNDED* PREDATOR WOULD *NOT* FOLLOW.

3

LATELY, THOUGH, HE HAS COME TO *QUESTION* HIS *JUDGEMENT.*

THE *ATTACK* ON THE STYRACOSAURS IS JUST *ANOTHER* EXAMPLE.

HE *REGARDS* THE *WOUND* ON HIS *LEG.*

IT'S *BAD.*

THE CERATOPSID'S *HORNS* HAD *RIPPED* OPEN SEVERAL *LARGE GASHES* IN HIS LOWER LEG, RIGHT DOWN TO HIS *FIBULA.*

THERE IS A *LOT* OF *BLOOD.*

HE *HAS* BEEN HURT *BEFORE*.

ONCE, IN A *FIGHT* WITH ANOTHER *ALBERTOSAUR*, HE HAD *DAMAGED* HIS *JAW* SO BADLY HE COULDN'T *EAT* FOR NEARLY *THREE WEEKS*.

SQUINTING THROUGH THE *PAIN*, THE *OLD DINOSAUR* NOTICES THE SKY FILLING WITH *HEAVY*, GREY *CLOUDS*.

A *STORM* IS MOVING IN. HE WILL HAVE TO *LAY LOW* FOR A WHILE.

WHEN HE *AWAKENS* THE NEXT *MORNING*, IT IS TO SEVERAL INCHES OF NEW *SNOW*.

IT WAS *NOT* AT ALL *UNUSUAL* FOR THIS REGION TO RECEIVE AN OCCASIONAL *SNOWFALL*.

STILL, THERE IS SOMETHING *FASCINATING* ABOUT THE *CHANGE* IN THE *LANDSCAPE*.

THE URGENT *ACHE* IN HIS *LEG* BRINGS THE OLD DINOSAUR BACK TO *REALITY*.

THE WOUND *BARELY* OOZES NOW, ALTHOUGH IT IS *STIFF* AND *VERY SWOLLEN.*

AFTER *CLEANING* IT, HE RAISES HIS HEAD AND *STARES* OUT FROM HIS HIDING PLACE.

THERE IS NO *MOVEMENT* OR SOUND.

IT WAS AS IF THE *SNOW* HAS CAUSED EVERYTHING TO *CEASE.*

THAT'S WHEN HE *SEES* IT.

8

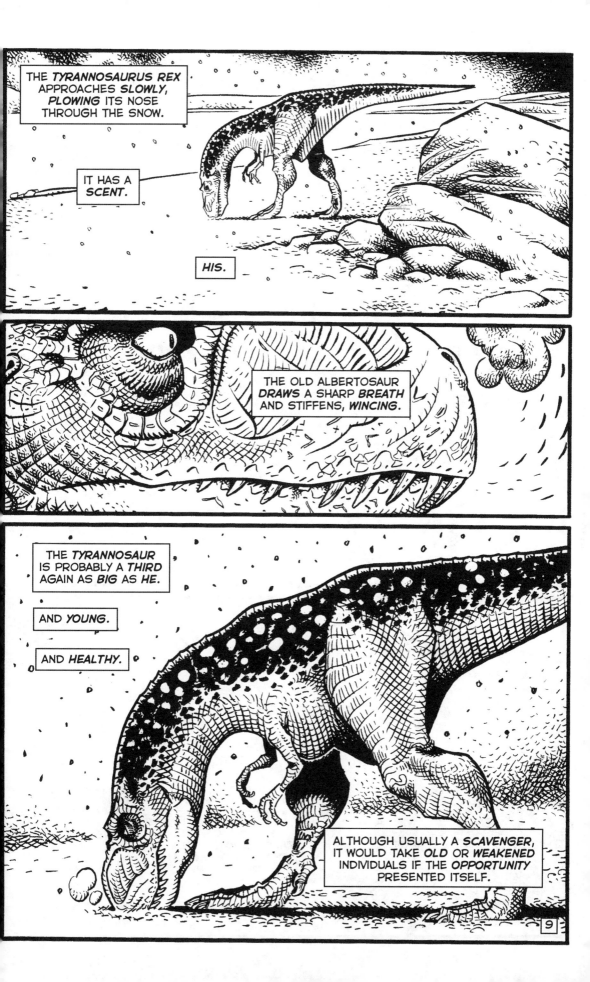

THE *OLD ONE* KNOWS HIS *ONLY* CHANCE WAS TO *BLUFF.*

ROLLING UP ONTO HIS FEET, THE ALBERTOSAUR *BURSTS* FROM HIS SHELTER, *TOSSING* HIS HEAD BACK AND FORTH AND *BELLOWING* ANGRILY.

THE TYRANNOSAURUS *STOPS,* UNSURE OF WHAT TO DO... HIS PREY'S *BOLD* CHARGE WAS *UNEXPECTED.*

BUT, *HIDDEN* WITHIN THE ALBERTOSAUR'S *THREATENING* ROARS, DOES HE *DETECT* A CRY OF *PAIN?*

10

THE BLUFF HAS *WORKED.*

IN A *SUBMISSIVE* GESTURE, THE TYRANNOSAURUS REX *LOWERS* ITS HEAD AND TURNS *AWAY,* AS THE OLD CARNOSAUR *HOLDS* HIS *GROUND,* CONTINUING TO BELLOW *DEFIANTLY.*

11

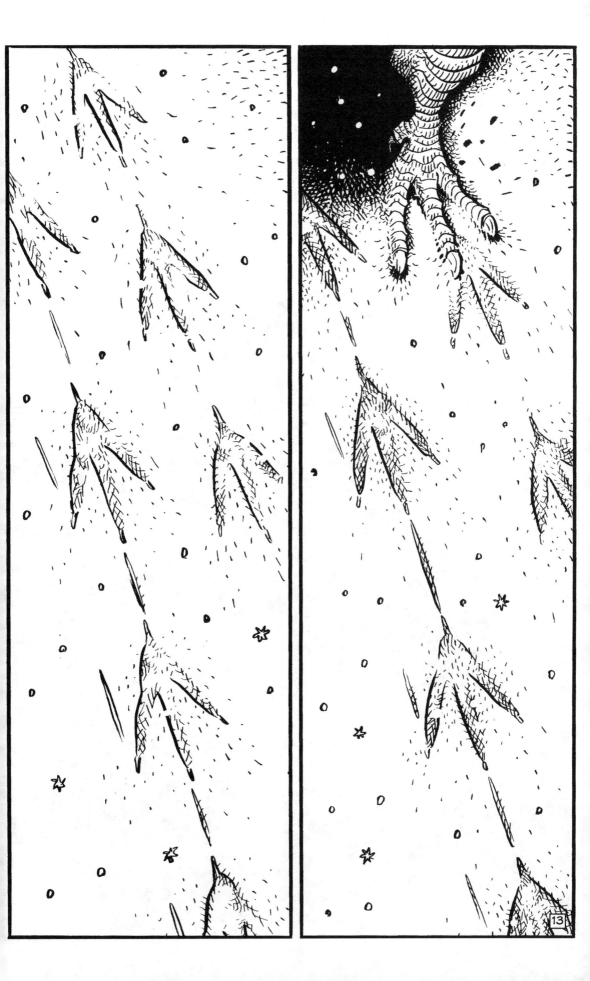

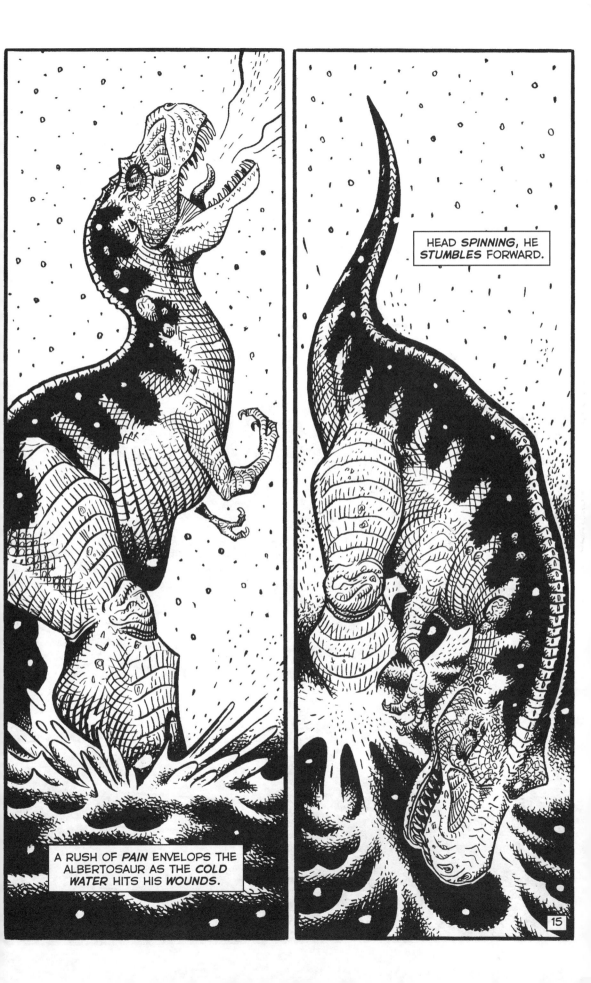

HEAD *SPINNING*, HE *STUMBLES* FORWARD.

A RUSH OF *PAIN* ENVELOPS THE ALBERTOSAUR AS THE *COLD WATER* HITS HIS *WOUNDS*.

15

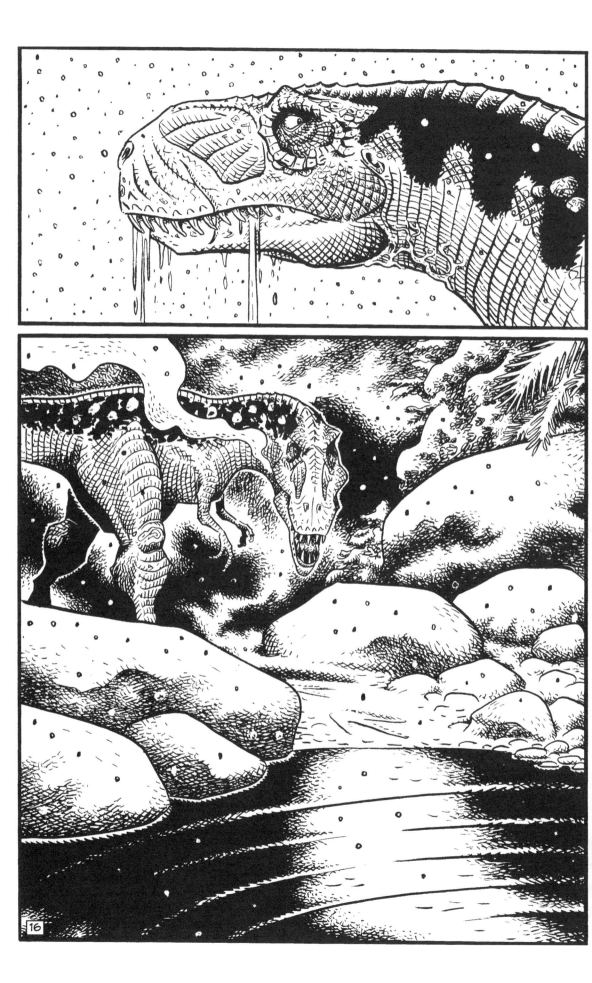

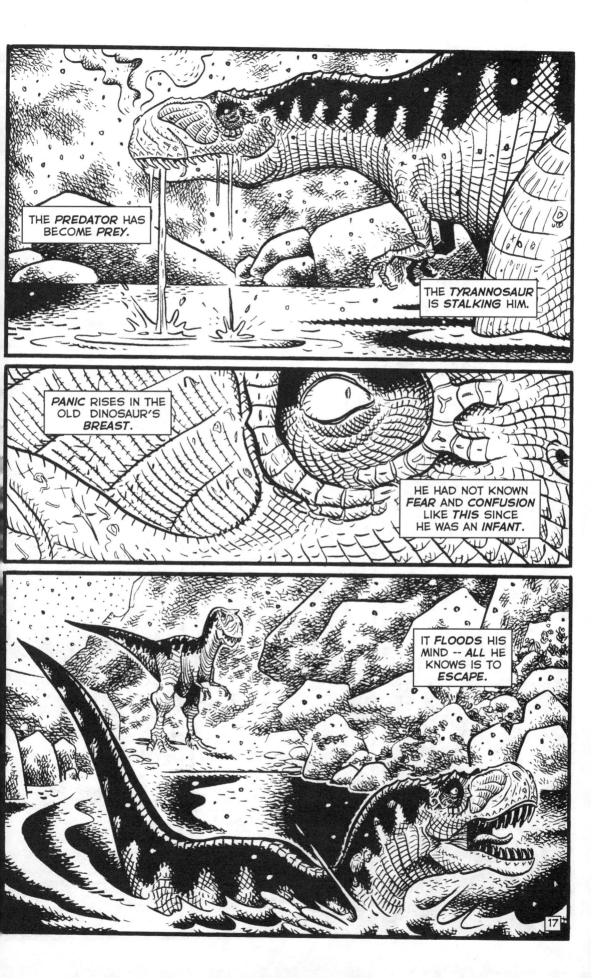

IT IS A *SHORT* SWIM TO THE OTHER SIDE. FROM *THERE*, ONLY ONE *WAY OUT* IS *VISIBLE*...

...UP A SMALL *RAVINE* CARVED OUT OF THE MOUNTAINSIDE BY THE *RAINS* .

THE *NUMBNESS* THE COLD WATER PROVIDED HIM BEGINS TO *SUBSIDE*, FLOODING HIS BODY WITH *PAIN*.

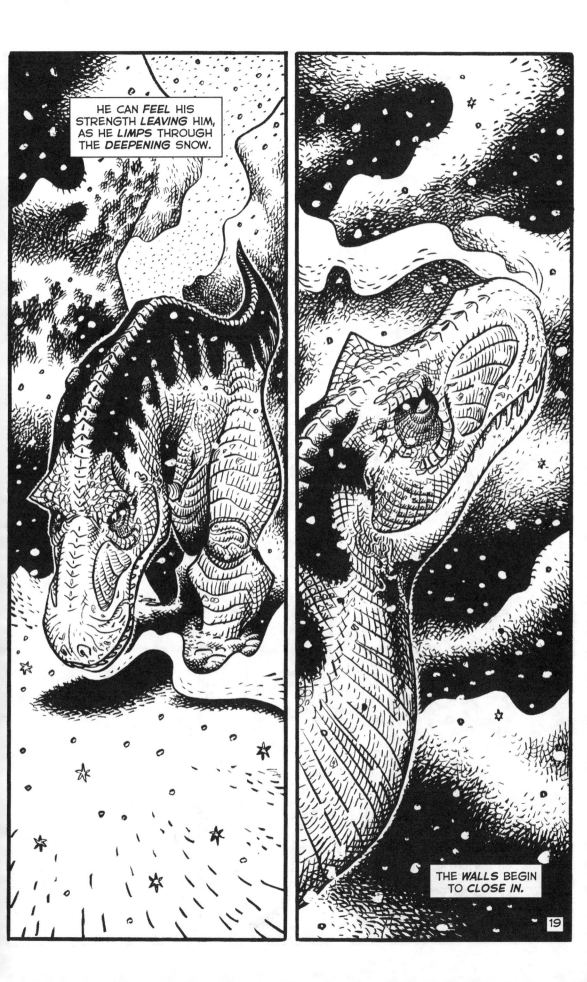

STUMBLING ON SOMETHING BENEATH THE SNOW, THE ALBERTOSAURUS SLAMS INTO THE SIDE OF THE RAVINE.

20

LEANING THERE, HEAVING, HE CANNOT WILL HIMSELF TO MOVE.

THE LAST THING HE HEARS IS THE HOWLING OF THE WIND AS HIS WORLD GOES WHITE.

THE TYRANNOSAUR *SQUINTS* AGAINST THE *WIND*.

21

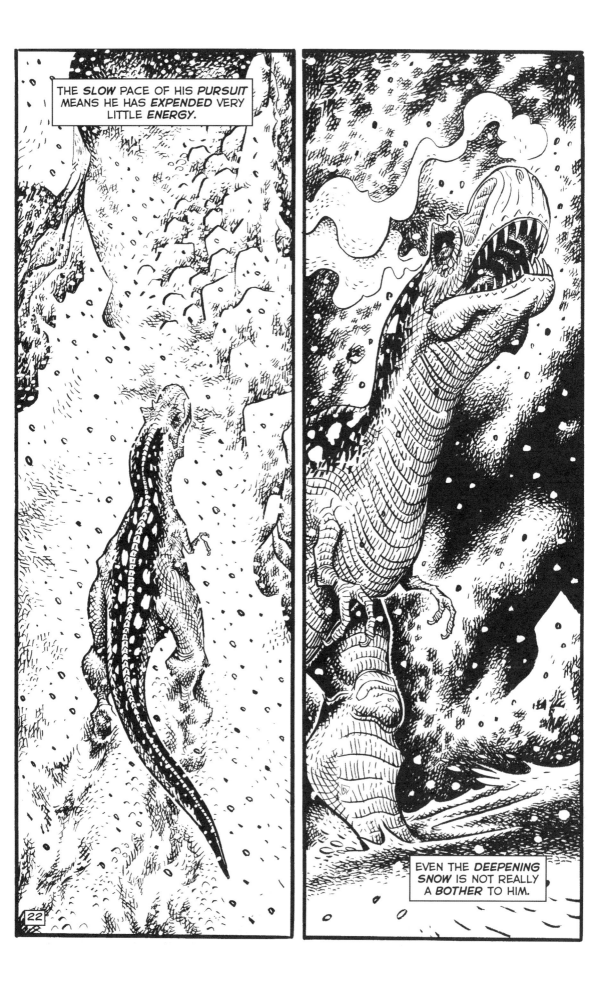

THE *SLOW* PACE OF HIS *PURSUIT* MEANS HE HAS *EXPENDED* VERY LITTLE *ENERGY.*

EVEN THE *DEEPENING SNOW* IS NOT REALLY A *BOTHER* TO HIM.

SOON, WITH HIS BELLY *FULL*, HE WILL *RETURN* TO THE *WARMTH* OF THE *LOWLANDS*...

...AND *SLEEP*...

23

THE OLD ONE *STARES* OFF DOWN THE RAVINE, *LISTENING* TO THE *GURGLING* AND *GASPING* OF THE FALLEN *TYRANNOSAUR.*

WAITING...

...UNTIL HE HEARS NOTHING...

...BUT THE SNOW.

HE *SNIFFS* THE BODY, THEN LIES DOWN *BESIDE* IT, IN AN EFFORT TO *ABSORB* SOME OF ITS *WARMTH.*

25

AS HE DRIFTS OFF TO *SLEEP*, THE ALBERTOSAUR NOTICES THAT HIS *LEG* DOESN'T *HURT* ANY MORE.

THE END

Book Six

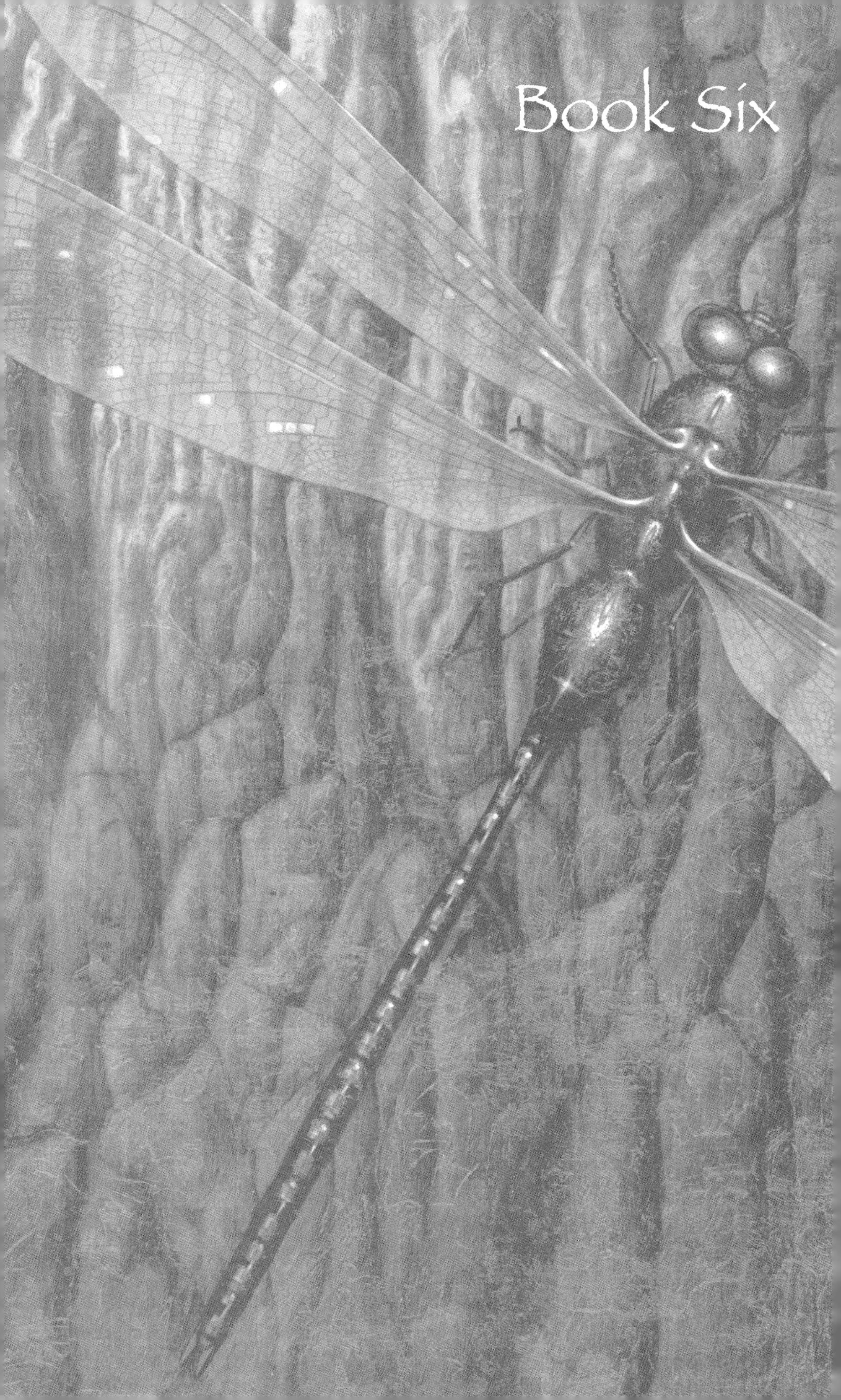

THE LUCKY AND THE UNLUCKY...
...THE EATERS AND THE EATEN.
ALL IS EVENTUALLY CONSUMED.
...AND TIME CONSUMES ALL.

THE MIDDAY *HEAT* HAD BROUGHT
THE *HERD* TO THE WATER'S *EDGE.*

THE *MUDFLAT* THEY HAD
CROSSED WAS *TREELESS* AND
EXPOSED, CAUSING SOME OF THE
CORYTHOSAURUS TO HUDDLE
TOGETHER *NERVOUSLY.*

THEY WERE
VULNERABLE HERE.

1

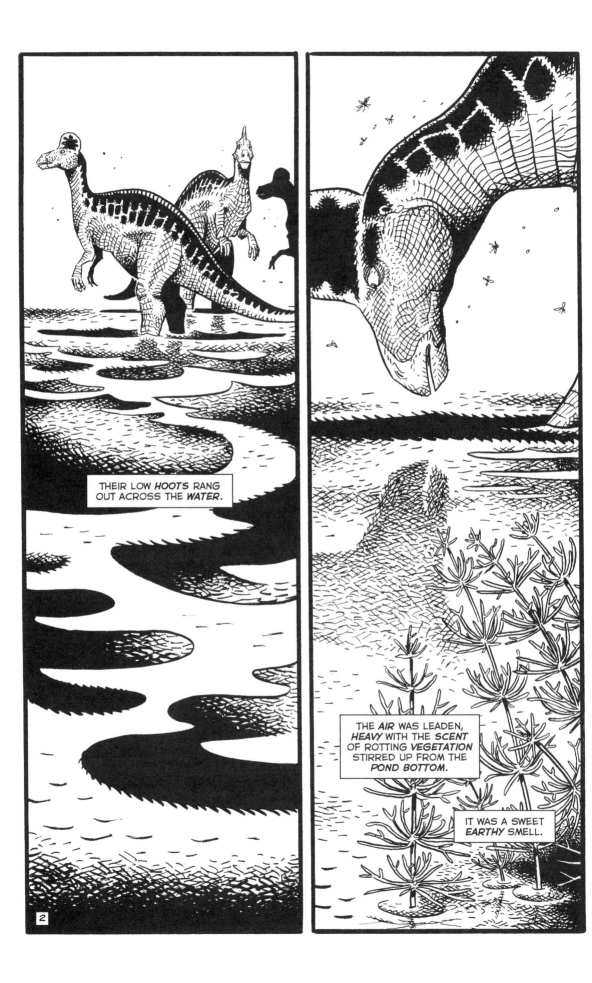

THEIR LOW *HOOTS* RANG OUT ACROSS THE *WATER*.

THE *AIR* WAS LEADEN, *HEAVY* WITH THE *SCENT* OF ROTTING *VEGETATION* STIRRED UP FROM THE *POND BOTTOM*.

IT WAS A SWEET *EARTHY* SMELL.

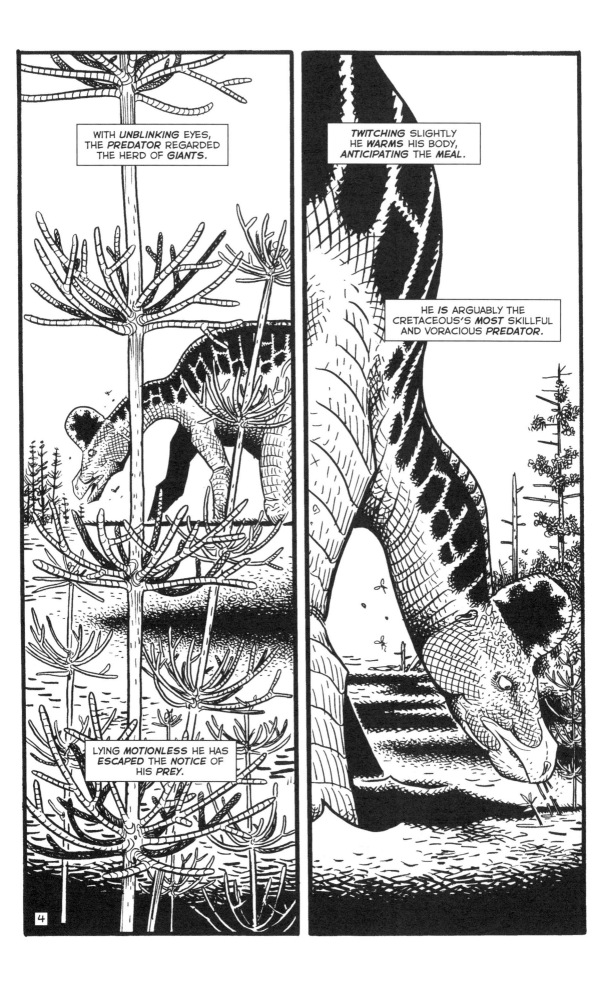

SILENTLY, REFLEXIVELY, THE HUNTER *BURSTS* FROM HIS *COVER.*

WHAT *CREATURE* HAS EVER BEEN *DESIGNED* WITH SUCH AN EFFICIENT, SINGLE *PURPOSE?*

INDIVIDUALLY, HIS PARTS ARE *IMPRESSIVE.* COMBINED, HIS PHYSIOLOGY MAKES HIM THE *PERFECT PREDATOR.*

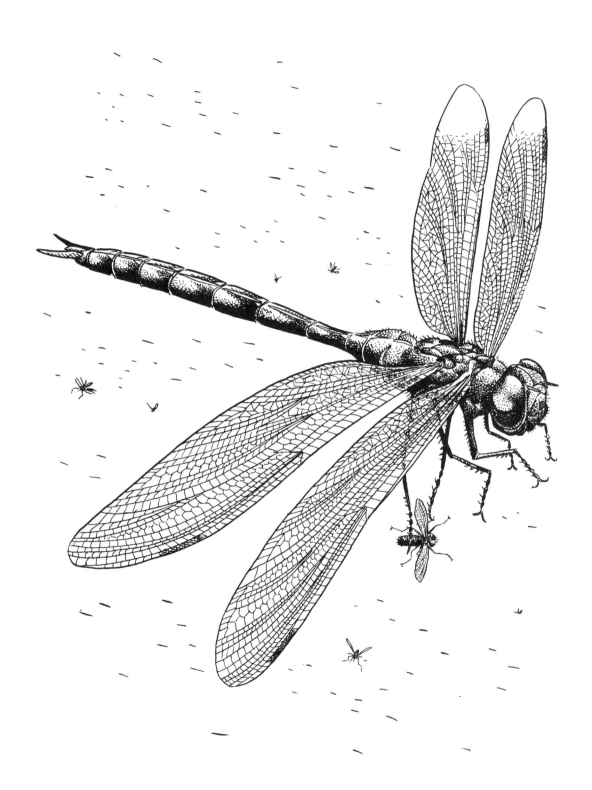

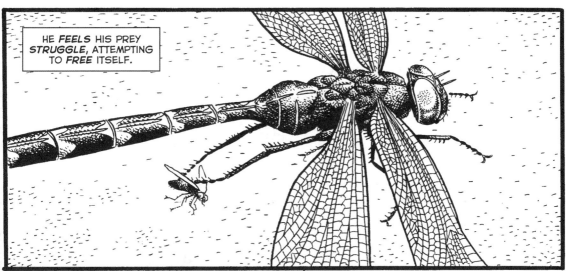

HE *FEELS* HIS PREY *STRUGGLE*, ATTEMPTING TO *FREE* ITSELF.

HE *TWISTS* IT FORCEFULLY, *BREAKING* OPEN IT'S *BODY*.

EXPOSING IT'S *JUICES*.

PASSING IT *FORWARD* HE BRINGS IT UP TO HIS *JAWS* AND WITH A *POWERFUL SUCTION*, INJESTS THE *BOTTLE FLY'S* INNER *MEAT*.

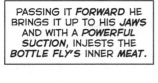

THE *HUSK* IS *DISCARDED*.

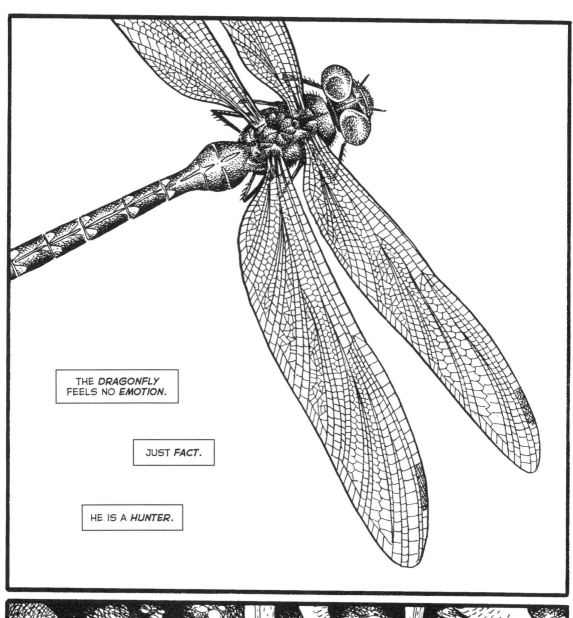

THE *DRAGONFLY* FEELS NO *EMOTION*.

JUST *FACT*.

HE IS A *HUNTER*.

THREE MONTHS AGO HE WAS A *PUPA*, LURKING IN THE *SEDIMENT* OF THIS VERY *POND.*

HE KNEW *NOTHING* OF THE *SUN* AND *SKY*. HIS *WHOLE WORLD* WAS A *TINY* FOREST OF *AQUATIC PLANTS.*

THERE, AMIDST THE *MUD* AND *SILT* HE WOULD *HIDE.*

WAITING...

EVEN AT THIS *EARLY* PUPAL STAGE HIS *WEAPON* WAS *FORMIDABLE.*

THEN THE HUNTER WAS BORN *AGAIN.*

ONE DAY HE SIMPLY *KNEW* TO *LEAVE* THE *WATER.*

10

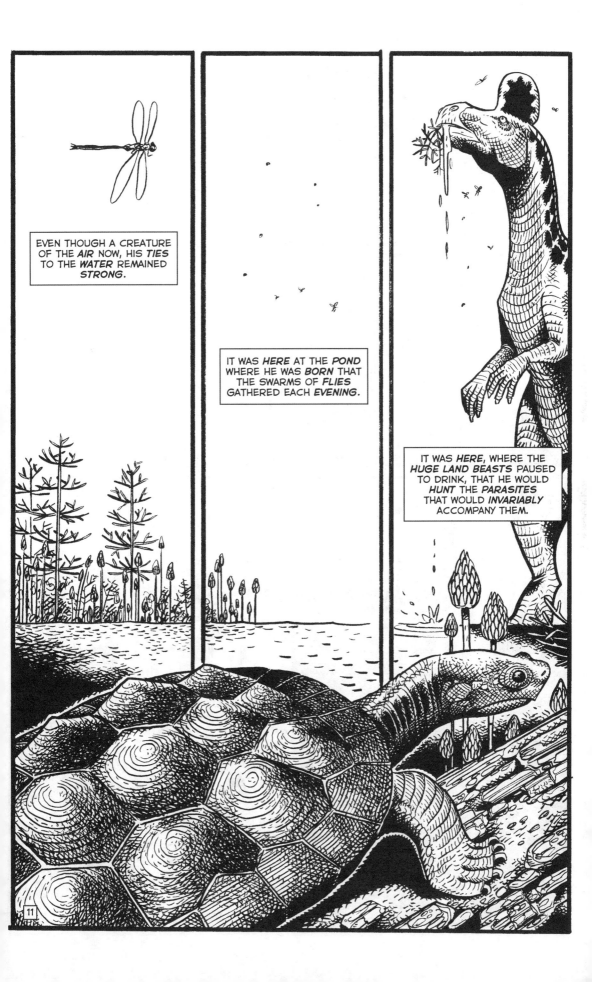

EVEN THOUGH A CREATURE OF THE *AIR* NOW, HIS *TIES* TO THE *WATER* REMAINED *STRONG.*

IT WAS *HERE* AT THE *POND* WHERE HE WAS *BORN* THAT THE SWARMS OF *FLIES* GATHERED EACH *EVENING.*

IT WAS *HERE,* WHERE THE *HUGE LAND BEASTS* PAUSED TO DRINK, THAT HE WOULD *HUNT* THE *PARASITES* THAT WOULD *INVARIABLY* ACCOMPANY THEM.

11

THERE WERE *OTHER* HUNTERS...

HUNTERS THAT *KNEW* OF HIM AND HIS KIND AND THEIR *BOND* TO THE *WATER.*

WHAT THEY *LACKED* IN *VISUAL* AND *AERIAL* AQUITY THEY MADE UP FOR WITH *SIZE* AND *INTELLIGENCE.*

12

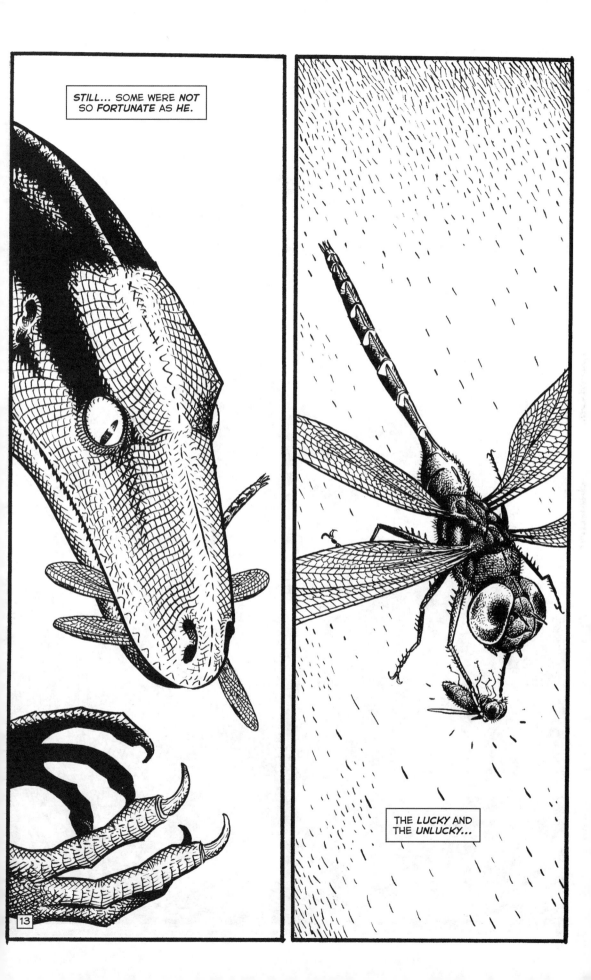

STILL... SOME WERE *NOT* SO *FORTUNATE* AS *HE.*

THE *LUCKY* AND THE *UNLUCKY*...

13

ALL IS EVENTUALLY CONSUMED.

15

TEMPORARILY *SATED*, THE DRAGONFLY TURNS HIS ATTENTION TO *MODULATING* HIS *BODY TEMPERATURE.*

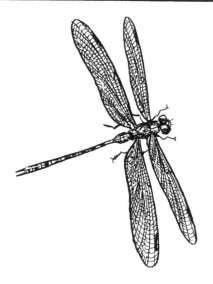

SHORT PERIODS OF *GLIDING* HELP TO *COOL* DOWN HIS BODY AND ALLOW HIM TO STAY ALOFT FOR *HOURS* AT AT TIME.

CHOOSING TO CONSERVE *ENERGY*, THE DRAGONFLY ALIGHTS ON A *TREE BRANCH.*

HE TAKES THIS OPPORTUNITY TO *CLEAN* HIS *MANDIBLES.* HE *SCRAPES* THEM WITH HIS *FORELIMBS* THEN *INJESTS* THE RESIDUE.

HAVING *FINISHED,* HE COCKS HIS WINGS BACK IN A *RELAXED* POSTURE AND TURNS HIS *ATTENTION* TO THE SUBTLE *MOVEMENT* ALL AROUND HIM.

17

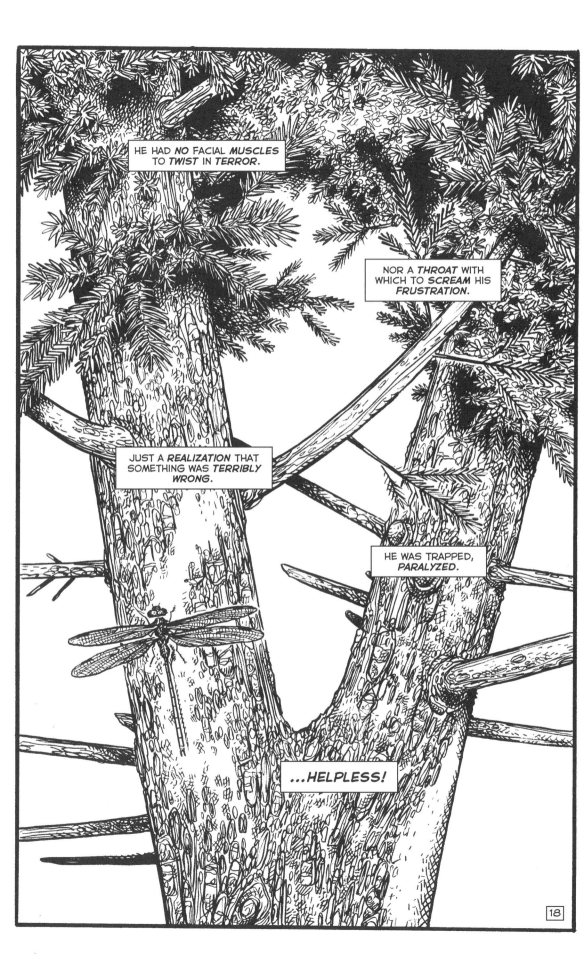

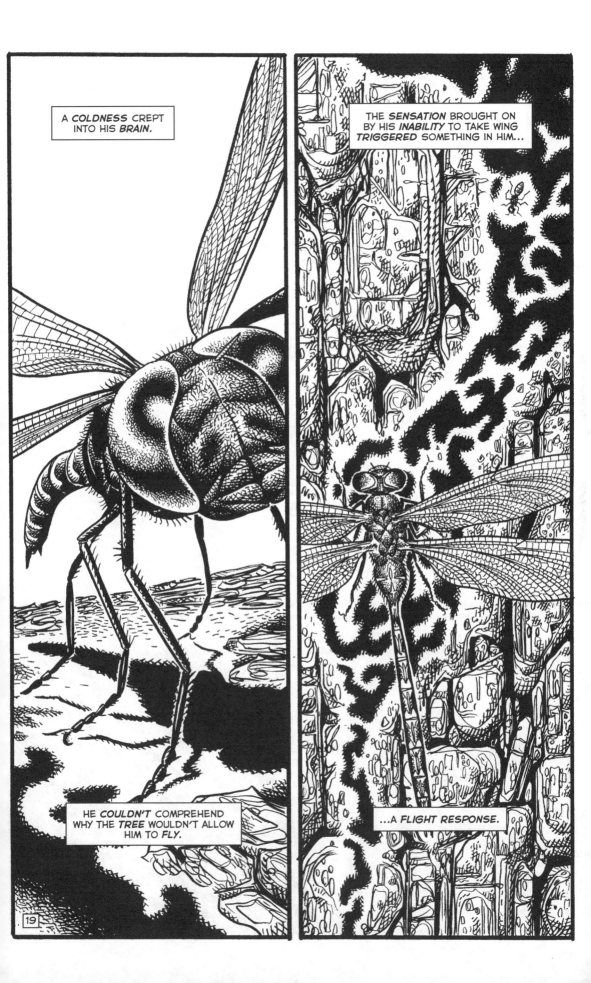

A *COLDNESS* CREPT INTO HIS *BRAIN.*

HE *COULDN'T* COMPREHEND WHY THE *TREE* WOULDN'T ALLOW HIM TO *FLY.*

THE *SENSATION* BROUGHT ON BY HIS *INABILITY* TO TAKE WING *TRIGGERED* SOMETHING IN HIM...

...A *FLIGHT RESPONSE.*

BEATING HIS WINGS *FIERCELY* THE DRAGONFLY *ATTEMPTS* TO BREAK *FREE*

BUT THE *DEEPENING* SAP WOULD HAVE *NONE* OF IT.

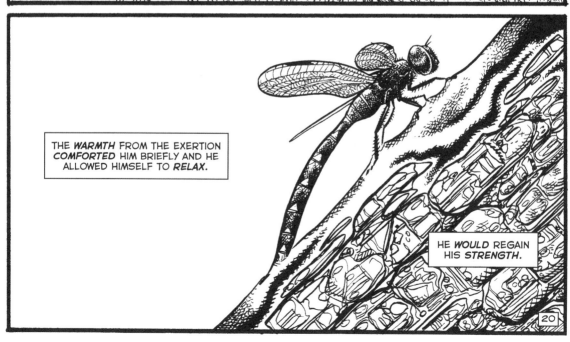

THE *WARMTH* FROM THE EXERTION *COMFORTED* HIM BRIEFLY AND HE ALLOWED HIMSELF TO *RELAX.*

HE *WOULD* REGAIN HIS *STRENGTH.*

20

STRONGER THIS TIME, THE COLD COMES CREEPING BACK.

BLINDLY NOW, REACTING ON PURE INSTINCT, THE DRAGONFLY SPASMS. URGING WITH ALL HIS STRENGTH TO BREAK FREE OF THE SAP.

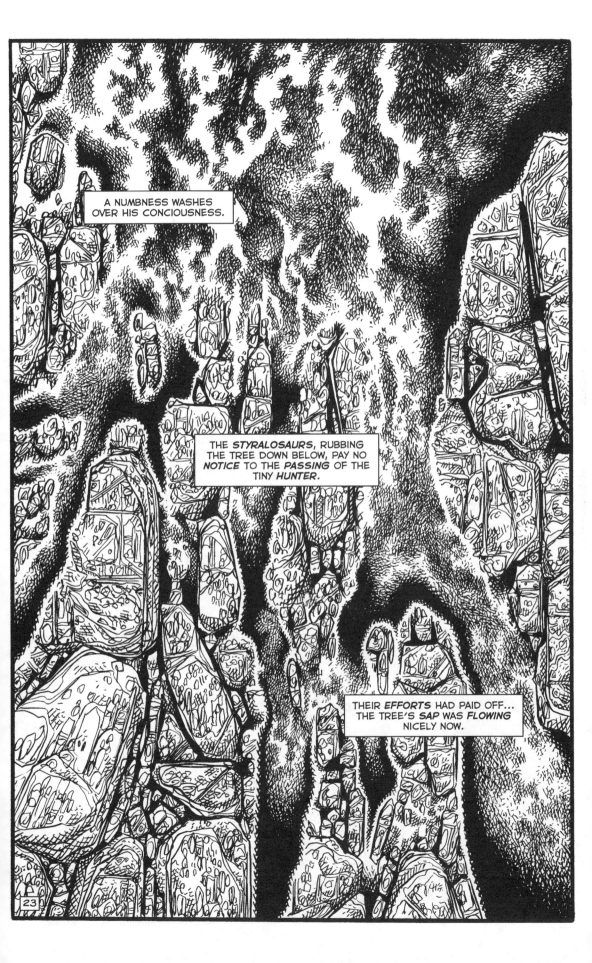

Bonus Material

DINOSAURS DIDN'T
COMPLICATE THEIR
RELATIONSHIPS WITH
SENTIMENTALITY.

2

3

4

5

THE
END